The THREE SURVIVORS

The THREE SURVIVORS

Snowflake

iUniverse, Inc.
Bloomington

The Three Survivors
Adventure Begins With a Giant Storm in 1832

iUniverse books may be ordered through booksellers or by contacting:

iUniverse
1663 Liberty Drive
Bloomington, IN 47403
www.iuniverse.com
1-800-Authors (1-800-288-4677)

ISBN: 978-1-4502-2254-9 (pbk)
ISBN: 978-1-4502-2256-3 (case bound)
ISBN: 978-1-4502-2255-6 (ebk)

Printed in the United States of America

iUniverse rev. date: 11/27/2010

"He has made everything beautiful in its time. He has set eternity in the heart of men; yet they cannot fathom what God has done from beginning to end."

Ecclesiastes 3:11

To My Dear Children

Jane and James

CONTENTS

Part 3 (1835–1837)

PROLOGUE

On October 10, 1832, a ship named the *Takaramaru* sailed from Atsuta to Edo (Tokyo), carrying one hundred tons of rice. It took two weeks to arrive in Edo, but if the wind conditions had been good, they could have made it in three days. Fourteen sailors thought they would come home safely as usual. But the strong wind and storms changed their lives. William Bligh drifted on the Pacific for forty-seven days; in *Life of Pi* by Yann Martel, a boy survived for 227 days, but the *Takaramaru*, a broken ship, drifted on the huge Pacific for 425 days. There was lots of rice to eat, but not enough vegetables. Because of the lack of vitamin C, many sailors died from scurvy. Fifteen-year-old Kenta, sixteen-year-old Kyu, and twenty-nine-year-old Iwa, a spiritually strong helmsman, survived. Seaweed, packed with vitamin C, and shellfish, which stuck to the ship, saved their lives.

At last, the ship reached land.

What kind of lives would be waiting for them?

This is based upon a true story.

Part One (1832–1833)

THE GLOBE

Where do I begin my story?

I was born in a tiny seaside town, Onoura, Japan. My father was a very honest man. He was a poor sailor, but I grew up in a warm environment. My parents spoke with gentle words. I thought I would live in this small town the rest of my life with Yuki, my fiancée. Yuki's name means *snow*. I still remember her beautiful smile and voice. My whole life revolved around her. She was as gentle as snowflakes from heaven; my very own spirit. How can I forget her?

The first time I learned about a huge sea, I was cleaning the storage room of my father's ship-owner, Genji. His granddaughter, Yuki, helped me clean.

"Do you want to see the world?" Yuki asked me gently.

"The world?" I asked.

"Open this box. See … this is a globe," Yuki said, and opened the wooden box.

"What? Is it a globe of the world?" I raised my eyebrows.

"Yes, the world is like a globe," Yuki said. "This place where we live is also on the globe."

"I can't believe it. If it is true, why does sea water not fall down from the globe? Even houses and people do not fall off the earth?" I asked.

"My grandfather said a globe is floating like a moon in the universe," Yuki said.

"I wonder why such heavy mountains, stones, and houses could be able to float. Our land must be flat. It makes sense to me," I said.

"I think so, too," Yuki agreed.

I didn't know where Japan was. I leaned toward the globe and turned it several times. "Oh, I found Japan," I said. But I was very disappointed. It was so tiny.

"This is Japan. I thought Japan was much bigger," I said and frowned.

"Yes, this tiny one is Japan, but Russia is much larger, and China as well," she said, smiling.

"What about this blue place?" I asked.

"This is the sea. A very big sea," Yuki said; she didn't know the name of the sea.

I wondered why the sea was so huge. I only knew that the Isewan Sea, near my home, was a large sea, but when I saw it on the globe, it was only a tiny dot. I looked with surprise at the sea that covered almost half of the globe. I never thought someday I would drift on this huge sea, an experience like a hell.

"This is America," Yuki pointed out.

I had heard the name *America* once before. "Do America and Japan connect through the sea?" I asked.

"Yes, also there are India, England, and more than twenty or thirty other countries," Yuki said.

"So many?" I dropped my jaw.

"This is a globe," she said and put it back in the box.

Since Yuki had helped me clean the storage room, I finished my job early.

"Thank you for helping me with the cleaning," I said.

When Yuki tried to dust a very old vase, she stumbled and it fell down on the ground. The vase was cracked. I picked it up, but there was no way to fix it. I sighed.

"This is my grandfather's favorite vase. He will be very angry. What shall I do?"

Yuki asked; her face paled.

Suddenly, we heard someone's steps.

"Oh, no, what can I do?" Yuki asked, holding her head with her hands.

"How is the cleaning? Have you finished?" Yuki's grandfather, Genji, appeared at the door. Then he looked at the vase that I held.

"What?" his eyebrows lifted and his eyes grew wide.

"I am sorry," I said and sat on the floor and lowered my head.

Then, Yuki shouted, "Kenta! Why are you sorry? I was the one who broke it."

Genji looked at Yuki. Tears wet her cheeks.

"No, I did. It was my fault … " I didn't want Yuki to be punished.

"No, Kenta. I stumbled and the vase slipped down. My fault." Yuki sobbed.

Genji looked at me and Yuki, one after another. His silence scared me. It lasted a very long time.

"Master, please forgive me." I knelt and touched my forehead down on the floor.

"Kenta, I told you everything in this storage room was valuable. Be careful not to break them. Do you remember?" Genji asked.

"Yes, indeed," I said.

"Then you broke one of my treasures," Genji said.

"Yes, sir," I said and waited for him to shout.

"No, Grandfather. I broke it," Yuki shouted.

"Yuki, shut up!" Genji said.

Genji said with a calm tone, "I blame for a small mistake, but I do not blame for a big one. You are already feeling regret. Your regret is punishment enough."

ONOURA, MY HOMELAND

My father was a seaman on a ship that carried rice to Edo or Osaka since he was eighteen. After my father became sick, my brother, sixteen-year-old Ichiro, worked on a ship named the *Takaramaru*.

I lived in Onoura, in a house half a mile away from the sea. I could hear the voices of children through the wind. They must have enjoyed swimming, but I had many other things to do. I had to wash my father's kimono, clean up lunch dishes and pans, and carry water from the well.

"Kenta," my father called weakly after he took his medication.

"Father, do you want to go to the bathroom?" I asked.

"Uh, sorry ... " Father said.

"It's okay," I said.

I came close to my father. He held my small shoulder and walked slowly. I felt happiness because he was still able to walk. After he had finished using the bathroom, I took him back to his futon.

"Father, the ships!" I said and pointed to the sea by the window.

"Oh, the ships came back?" my father asked and raised his head from the pillow. There were twenty or thirty ships. After the ships carried rice to Edo or Osaka, the captain returned with valuable special stones, wood, and bamboo that made the captain and the ship owners rich. Also if the ship was too light, it was dangerous. The sailors, like my father, were not wealthy, but nobody complained. They were satisfied to bring some money and souvenirs back and to see their families again.

"I think my brother's ship has returned. Can I go see?" My heart leaped when I heard the children's joyful noise from the beach.

"Yes, you can go," Father said with a smile.

I hurried outside and ran toward the sea. Every time a ship came to the beach, children swam to it. The sailors always gave us big salted rice balls. I licked my lips. I usually ate only wheat or millet.

When I passed Genji's house, I heard my sister, Hana, singing. She was only seven, but she was hired as a babysitter. Little Hana carried a big baby on her shoulders. I wanted to take her to the ship, but she still had to work. So I kept on running. Soon, my friend, Kyu, ran to join me.

"Ship came!" I shouted.

"Quiet. If many kids hear you, our food will be less," Kyu said.

"Ship came! Ship came!" I kept on shouting.

"It is not true! It is not true!" Kyu shouted, and we both laughed.

When we reached the beach, we took off our kimonos and swam toward to the ship. Soon, we were on the ship. We feasted on hot, delicious rice balls with salt.

~ ~ ~ ~ ~

Every day I took care of my father and helped my mother in the vegetable garden. But today, my mother stayed home and took care of my father, so I had time for school.

"Kenta, if you want to become a sailor, you must learn writing. If you don't know how to write, you can't become a captain," my father said repeatedly.

A captain had to write journals and exchange letters with merchants or government officials. I wanted to be a captain.

"Oh, Kenta, your handwriting is very good!" my teacher said and rubbed my head.

"Hey! Kenta!" Kyu said and smiled at me.

Yuki nodded at me, too.

There were only two girls in this school. Most of the girls went to the sewing school, but Yuki and Mariko, also a ship owner's daughter, loved reading and writing. We learned not only reading and writing, but also history, haiku, and mathematics. I liked to learn. I wished I could attend my school every day.

After school, we ran outside. It had been raining this morning, but the rain stopped and a rainbow appeared in the sky. Crickets chirped noisily.

"Won't you play a hiding game?" Kyu called to the children.

Everyone surrounded Kyu, but I hesitated. I knew I should go home.

"Kenta, are you going home?" Kyu asked.

"Yes, I am," I said and looked at Yuki, standing by Kyu.

"You should play with us once in a while. You always work."

"Kenta, play with us!" the other children chanted.

Yuki fixed her beautiful eyes on me.

"Well, okay, for a little while," I said.

Everyone gathered, and we played Rock, Paper, and Scissors. Kyu lost and became It. He stood by the big tree and covered his eyes with his hands. Children ran to hide under the veranda, inside a cave. In one instant, all the children vanished.

"Are you ready?" Kyu shouted.

"Not yet!" I answered. I forgot how to play for a while. When I tried to hide, someone was already there.

"Are you ready?" Kyu asked again.

"Okay!" a boy answered. I quickly opened the small storage room and slipped in and shut the door.

A hoe and a spade were hanging on the wall. There were stairs at the right corner.

When I looked at the stairs, I was surprised. Yuki sat on the middle of the stairs and looked at me. Her bare legs showed from the bottom of the kimono.

"Kenta, come here," she whispered.

I froze.

"Come here," she said softly.

We looked into each other's eyes. I felt I couldn't breathe, as if I had become a stone statue. I turned my head aside.

"I found Taro!" I heard Kyu's big voice.

"Saku! Jiro, I found you!" Kyu kept on shouting.

When I heard Kyu's voice, I felt relieved.

"Kenta, are you going to sail on the ship?" Yuki asked.

"Yes, I am going to," I answered.

"My father said you could be an excellent captain." Her gentle voice touched my heart.

Most of the captains were ship owners, but once in a while, sailors made captain, too.

"I am not sure whether I could be a captain or not, but I will try," I said.

"You can do it, Kenta! But you must not be a captain," Yuki said, and she stood up.

"Why not?" I asked.

Yuki stepped down from the stairs quietly, stood beside me, and said in a very serious voice, "Storms are scary. I wish for you to stay on land."

"On land?" Her concern for my safety touched me. My heart beat loud like thunder.

The door swung open.

"I found you!" Kyu shouted.

~ ~ ~ ~ ~

The sea was dyed multi-colored by the sunset: purple, yellow, red, green. I narrowed my eyes and admired the gorgeous sea. The sun fell quietly; softly, the sunset changed the sea into purple.

"Brother!"

I turned around; little Hana ran toward me.

"Hana!" I shouted.

"Brother, I got flounders," Hana yelled and ran in the narrow path between the fields. Once in a while, Hana received dried fish and seaweed as a bonus for baby-sitting. Every morning, Mother woke Hana up. Hana rubbed her sleepy eyes, went to the well and washed her face, and then went to work. She ate breakfast and lunch at Genii's house, so our family saved food, which was Hana's wage for baby-sitting. Once in a while, Genji gave her extra food as a bonus. My heart ached when Hana handed five flounders to me. Hana was only seven and she worked as a baby-sitter. I felt guilty, as I went to school and played once in a while.

"Looks delicious, Hana." I smiled and smelled the fish.

Hana nodded happily and ran into the house.

"Father! Mother!" Hana shouted. As she missed our parents, she wanted to see their faces as soon as possible when she came home.

"Oh, Hana, thank you," Father said, turning his face to Hana.

Mother ran from the kitchen and hugged Hana.

"Mommy ..." Hana said, half weeping. She stayed with the outsiders all day and felt like crying when she saw her mother's face.

"Mother, Hana got these flounders," I said and raised them higher.

"Oh, it is appreciated," Father said, and he joined his hands together.

"Yes, it is really a blessing, Hana. You work hard," Mother said and rubbed Hana's head.

"I will bake them for supper," Mother said, and she turned to go to the kitchen.

"No, Mother, I will cook. You stay with Hana," I said.

After the supper, Hana fell asleep as usual. A baby-sitter's job was extremely hard for a young child. But some children even younger than Hana worked like this. I picked up my tiny, soft sister with her sleepy, round face and laid her on the futon.

Suddenly, I heard a voice.

"Good evening. How do you feel tonight?" Yuki's grandfather, Genji, came in with a smile.

"Oh, master." My father tried to get up from the futon.

"No, please relax." Genji waved his aged, stained hands.

"Thank you very much; you always take care of my children. And also you gave us tasty flounders today," my father said and bowed deeply.

"Never mind; a ship owner and a sailor are like a family. I brought rice cakes." Genji offered the package to my mother.

My mouth watered. I rarely ate rice cakes. Once in a while, a monk gave me one when they had a ceremony.

"Thank you very much." My mother bowed and received them.

"Not at all. By the way, Kenta is a very smart boy, isn't he?" Genji asked.

I was surprised when Genji said my name.

"Yuki told me Kenta was the only one in the class who memorized the haiku that Ikyu the monk wrote," Genji said.

"Oh? Ikyu's haiku?" Father asked.

"Yes, 'If we were born everyone would die ...' Yuki was impressed. Kenta, you were the only one who remembered it out of thirty students," Genji said, smiling.

I felt as though a gentle breeze touched my cheeks when I heard Yuki was impressed with me.

"By the way, I would like to ask you a favor today," Genji said.

"Yes?" My father raised his head from the pillow.

"Be still," Genji stopped my father, and then he started to smoke his pipe. His face became serious, and he said, "I want Kenta to be Yuki's husband in the future."

"What? Will Kenta be Yuki's groom?" My father dropped his jaw; my mother's pupils became large like a full moon.

I will be Yuki's groom! I held my breath.

"Hmm ... indeed you are surprised, but this idea is not just a spur-of-the-moment idea," Genji said.

"But, master, our status is too different. We are poor sailors; it is too much," my father said and started shaking.

"Master, we appreciate the thought," my mother said.

"Listen. I was always impressed by your honesty and hard-working habits. Hana is a good girl as well," Genji said.

I shook too, and listened carefully to Genji's every word.

"I have never seen anyone work like Kenta. Even when he wipes the floor or cleans up the garden, he thinks very carefully and does not waste any time," Genji said.

Did I do as well as he said?

Genji continued, "When I asked him to do an errand, he asked me, if the person was absent, should he give it to someone else in the house or a neighbor?"

"But," my father shifted on the pillow.

"Wait! Listen. One day, I asked Kenta to clean up my storage room. I told him everything in the storage room was my treasure. I felt I could depend on twelve-year-old Kenta more than on a grown-up," Genji said with a smile.

"I am humbled by this great honor," my father said and lowered his head; he seemed to shrink when he heard Genji's words.

"But I had a visitor, so I was away from the storage room awhile," Genji said.

"Did Kenta do something wrong?" Father asked.

"Yes, when I came back to the storage room, Kenta held a broken vase and sat on the floor," Genji said.

"Did Kenta break it?" my father asked; his face paled.

I shut my eyes.

"Kenta asked me for forgiveness, but when I looked at Yuki, I understood it was her mistake. Kenta took the blame for her! But I did not let on that I knew, and I observed Kenta until night," Genji said.

"Ah …" Father sighed.

"I didn't shout at Kenta, but he must be depressed, I thought. But he had not changed his mood and worked normally as usual," Genji said.

"Hmm …" murmured Father.

"When I saw his good attitude, I felt Kenta is the one who should be my heir. Yuki has a brother, Kazuo, but he is not only very weak physically, but also spiritually; thus, he can't be my heir." Genji smoothed the sleeves of his kimono. "Well, when Kenta reaches sixteen or seventeen, will he be Yuki's husband? I would like to ask you permission for the engagement," Genji said and bowed.

My parents hesitated, but at last they accepted Genji's proposal.

Yuki and I were engaged to be married.

"Today is a happy day. Well, my son, Jumon, and his wife, Fumi, never disagree with my decisions. I didn't ask Yuki and Kenta, but I don't think they will refuse, right, Kenta?" Genji asked, looking straight at me. Then he laughed happily.

I blushed and lowered my head.

SAKE RACE

The mountains were filled with mushrooms and a field of pampas grass. One autumn day, October 1, 1832, the *Takaramaru* arrived offshore in Onoura. Usually soon after the ship dropped an anchor, a lot of packages lay on the bank. But this morning, a helmsman, Taku, lay in the boat because he had had a heart attack the night before. His son, Zen, a cook on the *Takaramaru*, stayed with him and looked at his father uneasily.

After Taku was carried to his house, the beach returned to normal.

Much lumber and bamboo sat at Genji's lumber yard. Lunchtime passed. Genji's sailors and helpers received sake and lunch at the big kitchen in his house.

Kyu talked loudly. "It was cool. We won first place. First place!" Kyu looked at me proudly.

Yuki served with the other women. Kyu had worked on the *Takaramaru* for a year. I sailed on the ship twice last year. Genji loved me so much that he wanted me to work for him at home.

"You will be fifteen next year, and then I will send you to the ship," Genji said, making an excuse to keep me near him.

Kyu was fifteen and I was fourteen, but Kyu had big shoulders. He looked like he was much older than me.

"First place. It was great," I said.

"Oh, cool. From Osaka to Edo, it took only four days. Usually it takes fourteen," Kyu said.

A man shook an empty sake bottle, amazed. "It was the new sake race!"

I nodded. The ships were filled with newly barreled sake. Before those new sake ships left from Osaka, many people sang along with a three-stringed *shamisen* and drum, like a festival. If the ship arrived

11

early to Edo, the merchants were able to raise the sake price. It normally took two weeks to arrive in Edo, but if the wind blew well, they might make it in three or four days.

Merchants especially welcomed the first arriving ship. The captain wore a red kimono and danced as he got off the ship first. Then all the sailors received special treats, such as sake, food, and money.

This year, the *Takaramaru* won first place. In order to win the race, the helmsman, Taku, worked extremely hard; thus, he had had a heart attack. Kyu couldn't understand that fact. He was just happy that his ship won.

"The sailor danced like this," Kyu said and stood up, and one leg rose higher. He turned his head sideways, and made a gesture with his arms. Yuki and the other women laughed. Kyu kept on dancing in triumph.

"Kenta!" Genji called, much louder than his usual calm tone. Everyone stopped talking.

"Yes?" I sat on the floor with my back straight.

Genji put his sake cup on the floor and asked, "Kenta, do you know our helmsman, Taku, is sick?"

"Yes, I know," I said.

"If you know it, it is all right; but if anyone in our family gets sick, you must not laugh loudly," Genji said.

"I am sorry," I said and lowered my head.

Kyu was the one who danced and made us laugh. But Genji blamed me. I understood why. He always taught me, *Your inferior's achievement is his credit, and your great victory is also your inferior's victory. But if your inferior makes a mistake, it will be your responsibility. Just like when Yuki broke the vase, you took responsibility. This is the secret of a great leader.*

I knew Genji wanted me to be a captain in the future. So he was strict with me, but I still didn't feel that I would ever be superior to older sailors—until this moment. When Genji blamed me in front of many people, I at last understood I would one day be a captain.

"Kenta, Taku got sick, and his son, Zen, can't sail for a while, so you must go on the ship instead of Zen. Everyone understand?" Genji asked.

"Yes, sir!" All the men bowed deeply.

"But I don't know who will be a helmsman. On October 10, we

have to carry rice to Edo. What can I do? I wish Iwa were here," Genji said, folding his arms.

"Iwa is a strange man, but he is an excellent helmsman," said Genji's son, Jumon. "He left the ship two years ago."

"We must ask Iwa. Does someone know where he lives?" Genji asked.

"Yes, I know," Kyu replied proudly.

"Kenta," Yuki came close, pulling my kimono sleeve and whispering. Her eyes told me to go outside, and then she left. I followed a little while later.

Yuki fidgeted by a camphor tree near the gate.

"Kenta, are you going to sail on the ship?" Yuki asked, almost crying.

"Why do you cry? I will be back in a month," I said.

"But ..." Yuki sobbed.

"I will buy you a souvenir. How about a red comb?" I asked.

Yuki shook her head. "I don't need anything. I don't want to separate from you, even for a month." Tears ran down her beautiful cheeks.

THE *TAKARAMARU*

All ships had a household Shinto altar. The ship, "*Takaramaru*," written in *sumi* (Japanese black ink) hung on the wall. Straw mats lined the floor. A storage room beneath the floorboards held plenty of charcoal and firewood.

I washed the rice and put it into a big iron pot. Then I poured water from a tank over the rice. Inside the full water tank, I placed charcoal, which protected the water from spoiling.

"The most important thing to a sailor is water. If you waste the water on land, you will be punished," my father said. I had heard it since I was a small child. So I always cared for the water. When I carried the water from the well, I tried not to spill even one drop.

On October 7, it was raining. Tomorrow, we would carry one hundred tons of rice in our ship. Some sailors went home and relaxed. Only Master Chef Goro and I worked onboard. Kyu was also a cook, but he had gone to Iwa's house with Captain Jumon.

What kind of man is Iwa? Does he shout, too?

I sailed on the ship twice last year; I carried rice from Onoura to Atsuta. When sailors worked, everyone worked hard, but when they drank sake, some of them started shouting. When morning came, everyone forgot the fight the night before. But I couldn't stand their shouting voices. My parents had never shouted at each other. I never shouted at my sister, Hana, either. My father said, "You shall not hit anyone. If you get accustomed to hitting, it will become a big problem." He also said, "Kenta, do you know the difference between animals and humans? Animals can't talk, but humans can. Animals fight each other, but humans must use words and talk."

I think my father is a wise man.

While I cut the daikons (white radishes), I remembered Yuki's beautiful face.

The night before, my mother and sister came to the beach to say farewell. Several other sailors' families were there, too. But I couldn't see Yuki.

"Work hard, Kenta!" my mother said. "Ichiro, you work hard, as well, and teach Kenta everything you know."

"Okay, Mother. You take care of my father and live happily ever after," Ichiro said.

"Ichiro, what kind of a greeting is that? As if I won't see you again …" Mother said and then closed her mouth.

"Well, it might be the last time we see each other," Ichiro joked.

"Ichiro, stop talking like that. Usually a man who says he will die, never dies," Mother said, laughing, and looked at me and my brother.

Kyu's mother came for the farewell and said, "Kyu, you are a clown. Do not fall off the ship."

"Yes, you are very wild," Kyu's sister said, laughing.

"I am a kappa (a water sprite). I can live either in the water or land, right, Kenta?" Kyu asked. He looked at me and jumped on a barge.

Where is Yuki? I looked around, and then I saw her face between some pine trees in the forest. She looked straight at me. I waved to her. She returned my wave. I wrote the number one in the air, and she did the same. Then she drew a circle in the air, and I did, too. These were our secret signs. One meant "only you," and a circle meant "be safe." As many people were in Genji's house, Yuki and I always used these signs as our childish expression of love. She watched me gently, softly, and tenderly from a distance. I was satisfied.

"Kenta, Yuki didn't come today. She is a cold-hearted girl," Kyu said.

While I was cutting the daikon, I remembered my sister, Hana. When the ship began to move, she shouted, "Brother!" and stepped down into the cold sea. I felt a different kind of love toward Hana.

What shall I buy as a souvenir for Hana?

I finished cutting the daikon. The rain slackened.

~ ~ ~ ~ ~

The ship was divided into stem and stern. The tiller was almost fifteen square feet and the rudder was twenty feet. We needed at least two people to move the huge helm. When the ship went into shallow water, we had to raise up the rudder. Yuki's father, Captain Jumon, taught me when I had a little free time, and he also showed me the ship's log. He was a very meticulous man. He wrote:

On October 10, 1832, the *Takaramaru* left Atsuta. Crew members were as follows:

Captain	Higuchi Jumon
Helmsman	Iwa
Commander	Roku
Lieutenant	Nimon
Sailor	Masa
Sailor	Kazuo
Sailor	Tai
Sailor	Shiro
Sailor	Sensuke
Sailor	Jiro
Sailor	Ichiro
Master Chef	Goro
Cook	Kyu
Cook	Kenta

His handwriting was beautiful. I still needed to learn some more kanji, which came from China, but I could read most of the letters. Captain Jumon smiled and put the ship's log into a special box, made with double woods, so if someone threw it into the sea, the papers inside would be safe.

~~~~~

"Take a break, Kenta," Kyu said. After finishing breakfast, the cooks had to prepare for the lunch. I finished the preparation for lunch, and then I began to clean the cabinets.

"You worked hard, so I can relax, but …" Kyu said.

I rinsed the washcloth and put it on the counter and asked, "But what?"

"If you work too hard, I can't be lazy," Kyu said.

"I am sorry. But it is my nature. I can't change it easily." I smiled.

We went to the deck. I looked at the sails. They were huge, and I felt as if they were falling on me. "How big are these sails?" I asked.

"I am not sure, but more than sixty feet," Kyu said.

"Hmm … " I looked at the sails again. Iwa-san passed by.

"Iwa-san!" Kyu called in a friendly way, but Iwa-san just looked at him and left.

"He is strange. He does not talk much and he rarely laughs." Kyu shrugged.

"Yes, he is different, but I like him," I said.

"Hmm, are you sure? You like everyone, don't you? Did you see his wife?" Kyu asked.

"Yes," I said. I still remembered his wife, Akiko. She was a very elegant and beautiful woman, like an iris; her eyes expressed sadness.

"She was a pretty woman," Kyu said.

"Yes, and she looked gentle," I agreed.

"Oh, she looked like Kawanon, goddess of Mercy," Kyu said.

"I saw Kawanon's picture before." *Akiko was a beautiful woman, but she had a different kind of beauty from Kawanon.*

"She was more beautiful than Yuki," Kyu said and looked at me.

"You can't tell yet. Yuki is only fourteen, not grown up, but Yuki is beautiful as well," I insisted.

"Hahaha, would you stop going on about how pretty your fiancée is?" Kyu said and poked my forehead with his finger.

"Iwa-san loves his wife very much, so he didn't want to sail on a ship anymore. Also, he has a son. He wanted to stay home with his family, but when Captain Jumon visited him, he said, 'Only one more time will I sail.' This will be the last time for Iwa-san," Kyu explained.

Yuki cried when I was going to sail. Iwa-san's wife, Akiko, must have had the same feelings as Yuki. All of a sudden, Yuki's face appeared, her face sad, her eyes dark like the midnight sea. "Yuki," I murmured.

~~~~~

"Port!" the helmsman ordered.

"Port!" two sailors repeated Iwa-san's order. The sail was one-third lowered. When the ship dropped anchor, it was already evening and the wind had stopped.

Kyu and I cooked in the kitchen.

"The sea was peaceful today, Kyu," I said.

"But one never knows what will happen tomorrow. Storms are very scary," Kyu said.

"Yes," I said, putting baked sardines on each plate. Cooked rice's sweet aroma filled the sailors' cabin. Lanterns hanging from the ceiling swayed right and left like a pendulum.

From autumn to winter, accidents occurred often; northwest winds blew from Russia. They were different from a typhoon, but this wind blew for many days.

I climbed up the ladders and went to the deck.

Iwa-san stared at the sky. "The stars shine too brightly! And the wind has stopped." He curled his lips.

"Iwa-san, why does the Enshunada Sea have a lot of trouble?" I asked.

"Hmm, the wind is too hard and the ship is not strong," said Iwa-san.

"I thought our ship was the safest ship," I said.

Iwa-san laughed slightly and said, "Three years ago, I sailed from Osaka to Ezo (Hokkaido). I experienced many storms. During each storm, I felt our ship's weakness. If big waves came, water penetrated the ship."

"Why don't they remodel it then?" I asked.

"The Japanese officials insisted on closing our country to all foreigners, including trade. Nobody dares go too far away with our ship. This ship is made for home waters," Iwa-san said.

~~~~~

When Iwa-san and I went to the cabin, everyone else was drinking sake already.

Iwa-san sat on the floor.

"What do you think about tomorrow's weather?" Captain Jumon asked and poured sake into Iwa-san's cup.

"What do you think, captain?" Iwa-san asked him back.

"I think it will be okay," Captain Jumon replied.

"I agree, too," Lieutenant Nimon said.

"Well, I think we better sail tonight," Iwa-san said.

"Tonight?" a sailor sighed.

"Yes, when the wind starts to blow, we better sail," Iwa-san said with a strong voice.

"Well, I will check the weather again," the captain said and left the room. Lieutenant Nimon and Masa followed.

We all were silent. We were concerned about the weather. We wanted to rest tonight. We had carried one hundred tons of rice in three days. Our shoulders ached, but if we slept well, our bodies would heal. The sailors had two shifts. Steering, unfurling and lowering the sail, etc. Our jobs were endless. We wanted to sleep well tonight.

Then Captain Jumon came down and said, "No wind yet."

"Well, we will stay in port tonight," someone cheered.

FUNADAMA-SAN

"Spread the sail!" a sailor shouted.

I looked up from sitting on a package. At midnight, the wind blew cold, so Captain Jumon gave the orders to sail. I had to wake up after sleeping a few hours. I was very tired but had to work the second shift. I had to relate the helmsman's orders to sailors of the tillers. The cook did not only cook but also had many other chores aboard the ship such as cleaning and caring for the sick.

"Kenta, you are still sleepy, aren't you?" Ichiro came close to me and asked. His job was to raise and lower the sail and also to drop and weigh the anchor. He did not have to work much at this moment.

"Brother, you must sleep now," I said.

"Oh, once I sleep, it is very hard to wake," he said and looked at the star dust as the stars increased. "Kenta, do you know about Funadama-san (ship god)?"

All ships had a Funadama-san. One day before sailing, the Funadama-san was set in the bottom of the mast of the ship by a holy ceremony. A box, four inches by six, held some gold, a pair of Japanese dolls representing a married couple, and some woman's hair, usually the ship owner's wife's. We called this Funadama-san, and believed it was the soul of our ship and would protect us.

"I know, brother," I said.

"Kenta, our ship owner, Genji, is a widower. So the hair was not his wife's," Ichiro said.

"Well, then is it Captain Jumon's wife's?" I asked.

"Don't you know?" Ichiro laughed. "Kenta, you will be a captain and Yuki's husband in the future, but you don't even know what is inside of the Funadama-san," Ichiro said.

Ichiro sometimes said, "I don't think you can be a captain."

I didn't like to hear that, but I could understand his feelings. He must have been jealous. I didn't argue with him. "Well, I don't know much. I don't think I can be a captain," I said humbly.

"Well, I didn't know until yesterday. Tai asked the captain whose hair was in the Funadama-san," Ichiro said.

"Hmm …"

"What do you think the captain answered?" Ichiro asked.

"I don't know," I said.

"Don't be surprised, Kenta," Ichiro whispered. "Yuki's hair, the captain said."

"Really!" I shouted. My heart beat so fast. I prayed to the Funadama-san every day, but I didn't know the hair was Yuki's.

"Our ship-owner, Genji, loves his granddaughter, so he used hers," Ichoro said.

I felt very happy, as if Yuki was near me. I remembered Yuki, who shook hand with me in the woods on the farewell day. I slept peacefully that night.

~ ~ ~ ~ ~

I awoke to a beautiful morning, and I cooked miso soup. When I opened the big wooden cover of the iron pot, warm steam surrounded my face.

"Well, before I eat breakfast, I better go to the bathroom," Ichiro said and rubbed his stomach. He went to the stern, which had the kitchen on the right side and the water tank on the left. Between the kitchen and the water tank was an open space. We put a board there and used it as a bathroom.

As the sailors ate breakfast one after another, our ship passed by the Irakodoai Sea, which was the most difficult to sail. When the ship's course and the tide were the same, it was easy, but if they were opposite, we had to wait until the change of the tide.

Fortunately, we passed through smoothly.

"Well, we are lucky. It must be on easy sail," Ichiro said happily.

"But the weather is changeable. We can't predict it," Master Chef Goro said.

"By the way, Iwa-san is an excellent helmsman, I think," Kyu said.

"Oh, Kyu, you could see, couldn't you?" Master Chef Goro said with a smile.

"Well, I don't know too much, but when he crossed the Irakodoai Sea, he used an excellent technique," Kyu said.

"No, it was just luck. The tide and wind were good," Ichiro insisted.

"I think so, too," Masa said.

Master Chef Goro smiled and said, "Ichiro and Masa, sailors must know the helmsman's difficult work. You have to be honest about everything."

~~~~~

"Iwa-san. I brought lunch for you." I gave him a rice bowl with three takuwan pickles and a little miso (soybean paste) on the tray. "Why don't you eat with us?" I asked.

"Hmm, this sea is my side dish. Also, the Enshunada Sea is very difficult. Our ship sails by looking at land. We can determine our position according to the mountains' shape and the land. But in this area, the mountains and the land are very low. It is very hard to know our exact position. So I have to watch out." He looked at me and asked, "Kenta, how old are you?"

"Fourteen. Iwa-san, do you have a son?" I asked.

"Oh, he is two years old," he said; his eyes became gentle. Soon, he finished eating.

"Well, I will bring a refill," I said.

"Oh ..." Iwa-san put the tray in my hands.

Storm

"It is getting cold," Captain Jumon said to Lieutenant Nimon.

"Yes." Lieutenant Nimon nodded.

The sky changed to gray; waves became high as afternoon arrived.

"Cloud!" Iwa-san shouted.

I looked at the sky. A small black cloud rose from the horizon.

"Oh, look!" Captain Jumon pointed to the cloud. Then the number of clouds increased rapidly.

"We must go back," Captain Jumon ordered, his voice high and strained. We all knew the danger of these black clouds. The stern edged toward the land. The black clouds increased as if they were demons.

"Thunder!" Captain Jumon and Lieutenant Nimon shouted. Lightning ran through the black clouds. We were all afraid of this thunder and lightning because they meant a storm was coming.

"Lower the sail!" Captain Jumon shouted.

Lieutenant Nimon yelled to other sailors, "A storm is coming. Lower the sail!"

A northwest wind blew the ship. The mast squeaked with an uncanny sound. A huge wave pushed our ship from below. Kyu slid down from the packages. Iwa-san ran to the stern. "Captain. It is too late!" His voice was intense, but the next moment, he held the tiller.

"Lower the sail!" Lieutenant Nimon kept on shouting, but the strong wind made the sail very heavy. The winds and waves battered our ship. Master Chef Goro poured water on the stove in order to prevent a fire. At last we lowered the sail by two-thirds.

"Drop the anchor!" Lieutenant Nimon yelled. Then a strong wind blew, and a huge wave crashed onto the deck. Thunder roared as if it would destroy our ship. I gripped the package tightly. Our ship slipped under the waves. When we dropped anchor, rain poured down.

"Huge wave! Lie down!" Iwa-san shouted. A twenty-foot wave came toward our ship. I lay down, but the wave broke over the ship and another wave hit us soon after that.

"Is everyone safe?" Captain Jumon asked, but his voice was carried away by the wind. Wind and waves washed over us, one after another, and buffeted the huge rudder.

"Masa, raise the rudder!" Iwa-san ordered, but his decision was too late.

Bang!

I thought my ship had been cut in half. Then I realized the strong waves had destroyed the rudder.

"Oh! God!" Iwa-san bit his lips, "Damn!" He hit the rudder.

"What was that sound?" Captain Jumon and Lieutenant Nimon rushed over.

"Captain, I am sorry. The rudder is gone," Iwa-san said.

"Rudder!" Lieutenant Nimon grimaced.

Captain Jumon said, "Helmsman, don't worry. We can build another rudder."

I looked at the sea; the rudder's broken pieces were drifting with the waves and hitting the ship.

At last the sail was down and only a mast stood on our ship. Thunder and lightning struck the mast.

"Dump the rice overboard!" Captain Jumon ordered.

If we threw away rice, the government officials would be angry when we returned.

But Captain Jumon said, "Unavoidable circumstances. We must throw away two hundred rice bags."

We dropped the rice bags, one by one, into the sea. We knew we might get punished, but it was an emergency. Without the rudder, the ship was rolled easily by broadside waves. Every time our ship rolled, we all fell down on the deck, then stood up and fell down again. Sea water penetrated the ship. We bailed the sea water over the side of the ship, but now sea water rushed in. As we threw away one hundred gallons of sea water, two hundred more gallons filled the ship. At first, the sea water was ankle high, but soon it reached up to my knees. The sea water was cold; my legs were numb.

~~~~~

The rain and wind worsened. Around 8:00 pm, our ship crashed into a rock, and we all fell down on the deck, soaked.

Crack! Crack!

"Oh!" the sailors shouted.

Crack! Crack! the rudder kept on hitting the ship, until the kitchen and the water tank broke off and sank into the dark sea.

"There's no more hope!" Ichiro said and got up from the sea water and cried.

"Don't give up! Keep on bailing!" Commander Roku scolded.

Lanterns from the ceiling vibrated. These lanterns didn't leak oil with any kind of vibration and gave off splendid soft light. We scooped sea water into our pails and threw it outside the ship, but more sea water kept on pouring into our ship. It seemed useless, but if we stopped, our ship would soon be filled with water.

"No more hope!" Ichiro cried again.

"Indeed! It's useless," other sailors said and stood in the sea water.

"It's not useless!" I said in a dignified voice.

"Yes, Kenta is right. We shouldn't give up!" Commander Roku said. We were all troubled by the threat and again scooped the water. The commander ordered me to change my position, and I climbed up to the deck with tottering steps. The wind and the waves attacked me intolerably. The ship moved up and down.

Then Lieutenant Nimon shouted, "Captain, we must cut down the mast!"

"What? Cut down the mast?" Iwa-san asked loudly.

"As winds hit the mast, our ship lists terribly," Lieutenant Nimon urged.

"But, lieutenant!" Iwa-san said and looked up the big mast, its top blanketed in darkness. "If we cut down the mast, we will not be able to hoist sail anymore."

"Shut up, helmsman! Right now the most important thing is whether our ship lists or not." The lieutenant's voice was highly-excited.

"Lists? I have never heard that our ship is listing. The wind hitting the mast is not much!" Iwa-san replied.

"You are a fool! We must cut the mast, captain," Lieutenant Nimon insisted.

"Well, let me think," Captain Jumon groaned. Then we all staggered as a huge wave hit our ship.

"Captain, I went to Ezo (Hokkaido) in a huge storm like this, but we didn't cut the mast. A storm only lasts for a short while. After the storm is over, how can we go home without a mast?" Iwa-san asked. His words irritated Lieutenant Nimon.

"Helmsman. Dumb! It is our custom to cut down the mast. Captain, please let me cut the mast!" Lieutenant Nimon shouted.

"Well, we have to ask god," Captain Jumon said.

A light like a flame flashed down, illuminating the angry waves. Then they disappeared into darkness.

"Commander, helmsman, we must cut our topknots," Captain Jumon said.

"Yes, we must!" Lieutenant Nimon and Iwa-san replied.

Cutting our topknots meant our hearts were sincere toward god. We went to the cabin and cut our topknots. When we had to make an important decision, we had a drawing to discover god's will. Then we all believed that the result was god's will and obeyed. Captain Jumon had decided to ask god's will because Lieutenant Nimon and Iwa-san had contrary opinions. The captain ordered me to bring a measuring box with a cover. I placed it in front of the captain. He cut two pieces of paper and drew an O and an X. X meant "cut the mast" and O meant "do not cut the mast." He put the papers into the measuring box and covered it. He prayed and then opened the household Shinto altar. He took a wand tipped with stripes of white paper, shook it right and left repeatedly, and prayed some more. The captain, the helmsman, the commander, the lieutenant, and I prayed. I had never prayed so seriously in my life. Then I felt peace in my heart. I remembered Iwa-san's words: "Without the mast, how can we sail?" I agreed with his opinion. The mast was huge, but not much wind hit the mast. *I hope we don't have to cut the mast. God, please give us the right answer.* I was scared, but I realized my responsibility as a future captain, and that made me calm down. I prayed hard. We sometimes trembled on the floor, but I felt the storm weaken—maybe because of our prayer.

Then Captain Jumon lifted the measuring box and drew.

"This is god's voice," the captain said and held one paper high. We all bowed. I held my breath. "God's will is to cut the mast," he said solemnly.

"Oh …" we rubbed our heads on the floor. I looked at Iwa-san; he bit his lip.

~ ~ ~ ~ ~

The wind was still strong, but the rain slackened. I took the lantern and stood by the mast. Captain Jumon held the lantern. The ship rocked, and the mast squeaked. I couldn't stand up straight. *Is it possible to cut the mast?*

Captain Jumon ordered Iwa-san to cut the mast first. Iwa-san put the life rope around his waist and held on to an ax. His cheeks moved, and then "Ei!" He shouted with spirit and brought the ax down on the mast.

Kapow! a strong wind blew him.

"Watch out!" Captain Jumon shouted.

As Iwa-san raised the ax again, a huge wave hit him. He spread his legs and held himself strong, waiting between the ship's rocking motion. "Ei!" He brought the ax down again. The ax only glanced the mast. Once again he raised the ax. Wind blew him off-balance. We all stumbled and watched Iwa-san.

While Iwa-san chopped at the mast, other sailors continued to bail.

"Oh, at last the rain has stopped," Captain Jumon murmured.

After one hour or so, Masa said, "I will take over now." He received the ax from Iwa-san. Iwa-san's hair stuck to his forehead with sweat. I looked at him admiringly. Iwa-san sat down on the floor and breathed heavily. Captain Jumon ordered Iwa-san to cut the mast first; it must have been the captain's goodwill.

Young Masa was full of energy, but he trembled when he held the ax. Nevertheless, he tried hard. He slipped down many times. Cutting a huge tree was difficult work even on land. Now we had to cut the huge mast with wind and waves attacking. It must be a hundred times harder than on land. Before one hour passed, Masa was worn out. Then Lieutenant Nimon received the ax. Then Iwa-san tried again. The captain ordered us to wrap the ship rails with futons to protect them from damage when the mast fell.

The wind weakened, and the lightning diminished; nevertheless, the waves still crested high and were endless.

Now, Kazuo held the ax. He seemed exhausted; his cheeks were hollow. He had been working without food since the storm arose. Moreover, he was scared. It was a miracle we all had energy to work. I hadn't eaten for a long time, but I was not hungry. After Kazuo, Sensuke tried. Every time the ax came down, broken pieces of the mast fell down into the darkness.

Five hours passed. Captain Jumon and Iwa-san stood at the stern to cut the rope that hung from the top of the mast to the stern. In order to cut the rope, we needed good timing. When the wind blew the cutting end, the mast would blow down from the wind pressure. We must cut the rope at that very moment. If it were too early or too late, we didn't know in which direction the mast would fall. The ship rocked. The captain gripped his sword in his right hand, waiting. Suddenly, a few sailors shouted, and I saw their shadows move. Iwa-san grabbed the captain's hand without a word. "What are you doing? Are you crazy?" Captain Jumon said. His voice sounded hollow. He looked at Iwa-san.

The next moment, Iwa-san shouted, "Right now, captain!"

The captain swung his sword. The rope was cut perfectly. It jumped in the air, and the mast sunk into the angry waves.

"Wow!" the sailors shouted.

The captain sank to the floor.

"Excellent!" Iwa-san said and sat on the floor, also.

Captain Jumon didn't open his mouth for a while. At last he asked, "Helmsman, why did you hold my hand?"

"I am sorry, but at that moment, the wave raised our ship. When our ship was so high, it was very dangerous to cut the rope," Iwa-san said.

"Waves? I didn't recognize that, as I forgot myself. If I had cut down the rope at that moment, the mast would have fallen on the ship. Thanks, helmsman," Captain Jumon said.

"Well, it was your fine performance!" Iwa-san said quietly.

Now, we were all without the mast and felt empty. We never thought we would lose such a valuable thing. We all worked under the mast. Sometimes we lowered the sail, but the mast remained at the center of our ship. We dedicated the Funadama-san beside the mast.

I gazed into the darkness. Our ship was not able to spread sail anymore. *Will we go home again?*

Captain Jumon ordered, "Remove the sea water."

Sailors stood up slowly. Our job now was only to bale the sea water. It came up to my knees.

~ ~ ~ ~ ~

For five days and four nights, we fought with the storm, but by November 15, the storm relented.

Sailors brought wet firewood to the deck. Everyone wore a waterproof coat, tied with a rope around the waist. All our clothes were wet, so we had to dry them before we used them again.

We hadn't slept much for five days, but everyone felt relieved. The bright sun dazzled us.

"The sun is very welcome!" Kyu said, spreading the firewood on the floor.

"Indeed. The rain and wind have stopped," I said.

Our ship, the *Takaramaru*, was now pitiful—rudderless, mastless— but the blue sky and the warm sun gave us new strength.

"The Funadama-san saved us," Kyu said with a smile.

"I think so, too," I said. The Funadama-san must protect me as long as Yuki's hair was there.

"Wet!" Ichiro brought his kimono to the deck.

"Wring the kimono out and hang it over the side of the ship," Kazuo said while he squeezed his own kimono out.

"But even if we dry out our kimonos, we don't know when the storm will come again," Ichiro said.

"Stop complaining! Better to dry them out," Kazuo said.

"We will be wet again. I hate storms," Ichiro said and stood still on the sodden ship.

I felt sad, but I said to him, "Brother, the storm is gone. We must be happy."

"Don't you talk big?" Ichiro squeezed out his kimono and stood by the side of the ship.

"Oh, Ichiro. Did your brother give you a lesson?" Masa laughed and spread the fire wood on the floor.

"Masa, you kept on saying, 'Help!' and saying an invocation of Amida: 'Namu Amida Butsu,'" Ichiro said.

"Oh, Masa cried, 'Pa! Ma!'" Tai said.

Everyone offered some comment.

The first two days in the storm, we had all worked in rhythm. We had no time to talk, but we were like one body and one soul. Even though the strong winds attacked our bodies and we were soaked with icy cold sea water, we worked at our best. We were never hungry or sleepy, but after the second night, fear and anxiety crept in. We fought to stay awake. The fourth day, several sailors cried, "Dad! Mom! Help me! Namu Amida Butsu." Some called for god's help and cried. Masa hugged Captain Jumon and cried out, "Captain, please let me go home! I want to go home!"

Everyone was frightened except Iwa-san. He didn't change his facial expression.

"Helmsman! Will we survive?"

"Helmsman! How long will the storm last?"

Everyone started asking him, and he replied, "When the time comes, we will be okay," or, "The wind will stop when the right time comes."

His answers were not definite, but everyone depended on him.

Lieutenant Nimon was calm as well. He said, "Do not cry, okay!" He spoke abruptly, but with warmth and authority.

Captain Jumon was stressed because of his responsibility. He lacked decisiveness.

Master Chef Goro didn't ask for god's help, but he worked methodically. Our ship always had dried rice for an emergency, but he also prepared pickled plums. When the storm started, he made baked miso, which gave us energy. He moved twenty rice bags to another cabin, so the rice wouldn't get wet from the sea water.

We were surprised about Commander Roku, who had the most wisdom on our ship. He was excellent with an abacus and he had read many books. He wrote haiku. He was very resourceful. I thought he would be calm in any circumstance, but on the third day, his back became round like a turtle and he tottered on the deck. Now he lay on the wet futon and slept.

At lunch time, we ate warm rice. The water tank was gone, but we still had several water barrels. While it was storming, we had soaked the dried rice and ate it cold. But now the warm rice was so delicious.

KUROSHIO CURRENT

Where are we? Is that Japan? I remembered the globe that Yuki showed me in Genji's storage room. The sea was not flat but rounded. I didn't feel any wind, but this dusty purple sea was the Kuroshio Current.

"Helmsman, which way is Japan?" Captain Jumon asked with his dried, old man voice.

"Oh, I think that way," Iwa-san answered.

Most of us regretted that we lost the mast, but Iwa-san didn't say anything about it.

Our ship was on the Kuroshio Current, but we didn't feel the flow too much because the ocean was very big. We all believed that if we made a new sail, we could go home. We made a ten-foot sail, but it sat in the bottom of the ship, so it was only eight feet from the deck. The mast that we cut down was sixty feet. Our new sail was less than half the size of the original.

"Can we go home?" Ichiro asked.

"Of course. If the east wind blows, we will go home," Masa said joyfully.

"We need a sail in order to get away from the Kuroshio Current," Iwa-san said; he used a board from the stem and started making the rudder. "I want to go back to Japan. As long as I have the rudder and a sail, I will make it."

Everyone had hope. Even Commander Roku got up and came up to the deck and looked at the new sail.

It was getting dark, and stars shone. I felt Yuki was near. I smiled, then I went to the cabin. Soon I fell asleep soundly.

~~~~~

I lowered a pail with ropes into the emerald green sea and remembered the well in my backyard at home. *Splash!* The well bucket

31

would echo and the reflection would scatter. But this pail made no sound. I felt something heavy and jerked the rope. I stood firm and held my breath. There was another pail that had rice inside.

"Oh!" My brother, Ichiro, came and helped me pull the rope.

"Thanks, brother," I said. This was the first time he showed me such kindness. I poured one-fourth of the sea water into the rice pail and started washing the rice. The water smelled salty; soon the water became white. Then I poured the white water into the empty pail. I washed the rice again.

"Kenta," Ichiro called me.

"What, brother?" I asked.

"Our water tank is gone. It was a shame to lose it," Ichiro said.

"Yes, indeed," I said.

The hull of the ship was gone, along with the kitchen and the water tank, which was full of water. Fortunately, there were extra water boxes in the storage area. If we didn't have them, we would have been very thirsty by now. We were lucky, but the extra water was limited. "When you wash the rice, we must use sea water," Master Chef Goro ordered.

I had been washing the rice with sea water since. Every time I washed the rice, it sounded like *shaki, shaki.*

"Kenta," Ichiro called me again. "If we have no more water, we will all die," Ichiro said in a low voice.

"Hmm ..."

"Soon or later, we will have no more water. Then what?" Ichiro asked.

"Well, what shall I do?" I asked.

"We will all die." Ichiro grimaced.

I shivered. "Brother. Don't worry. It will rain, and we can make water by boiling sea water," I said.

"Yes, we can boil the sea water and use distillation. But if we run out of the firewood, what shall we do?" Ichiro asked.

"We will reach land by then," I said.

"You are a fool, Kenta. You must steal and hide water," Ichiro said.

"Steal?" I gazed at Ichiro.

"Of course. Even a cup of water. You better hide it somewhere." Ichiro lowered his voice.

"Brother, if our father knew, he would cry," I said.

"Yeah? He won't know. But if we die, Father and Mother will cry. And Yuki will cry!" Ichiro said.

"God watches everything we do. Water is important for everyone," I said and threw away the sea water in which I washed the rice. When I looked back, Ichiro was gone.

I carried the washed rice to the stove.

"Oh, did you wash the rice? Thank you," Master Chef Goro said and took the pail to get the water from the water box. This job was only Master Chef Goro's responsibility. This water box had a key.

Soon he brought over pure water and poured it into the rice pot. I looked at the water. *Steal the water!* Ichiro's words made me scared.

"Kenta, why don't you take a break?" Master Chef Goro asked.

"Yes," I answered.

If we have no more water, what shall we do? I wondered.

But we will have rain, and someday, we will reach land, I encouraged myself. I had always thought there were many little islands on the sea. Once Yuki showed me the globe, but I didn't understand that the Pacific Ocean was very huge. All the sailors believed we would reach some island sooner or later.

"Kenta, will you help us?" Shiro called to me.

"Kenta was just taking a break," Master Chef Goro said, but Shiro ignored his words.

"Kenta, I will be waiting for you," Shiro said.

I went to the hold of the ship.

"Oh, here you are. Scoop the sea water," Lieutenant Nimon said.

"Yes, sir." I scooped the water with Ichiro and Kyu.

"Kenta, come here," Lieutenant Nimon called me. "Kenta, sea water comes from here. We put rags into this tiny open space to prevent the penetration of the sea water, but the important key is the loose nails. I will teach you the places where sea water penetrates."

"Yes." I bowed my head.

"Kenta and Kyu are young and strong, so you must know everything …" Lieutenant Nimon said.

I felt a dark premonition from his words, as if he wanted to teach me everything he knew before he died.

"The place that sea water penetrates is called the sea water path.

So we have to find the sea water path as soon as possible," Lineament Nimon said.

Shiro, Jiro, Tai, and Kyu all nodded.

"Lieutenant, if we divide it, it will be easy to find the sea water path," I said.

"Oh, that is a good idea. The bottom of the ship is very huge, so once the sea water penetrates, the water wets the entire floor. But if we have dividers, it will be easy to find where the sea water comes in. We will ask the captain to make dividers," Lieutenant Nimon said happily.

"Indeed! Indeed! If we had dividers, water would come in only one place. Kenta, you have super ideas," Jiro said, smiling.

I was glad they liked my ideas. I worked hard to scoop the sea water. Water was tremendously important. Sea water was scary, and a lack of pure water was terrifying as well.

Someone made a noise. *What is happening?* I wondered and climbed up the ladders.

"What is going on?" I asked Master Chef Goro.

He turned his head and said, "Island! We saw an island."

"Island!" I felt dizzy and then shouted, "Wow! Captain, we saw an island!" and ran up to the deck.

Sailors pointed ahead and shouted, "It must be an island!"

"Is it really?"

"Of course, it must be."

"Is it a ship?"

"If it is a ship, we would see sails."

Everyone was very excited. The wind was calm, but we were in the middle of the big sea; when the swells became large, we could see the island, but when the swells dropped our ship to a low position, the island was gone.

"Which island is it?"

"I am sure it is not Japan."

"Russia?"

While Iwa-san heard everyone talking, he looked at the blue shadow intensely.

Captain Jumon asked Iwa-san, "Helmsman, what do you think? Is that an island?"

"Hmm, it looks like an island and also like a cloud. But I believe it is a cloud," Iwa-san answered quietly.

"Hmm … cloud," Captain Jumon said and nodded.

"What! Cloud? It is not true!" sailors shouted.

"Helmsman, why do you think it is a cloud? It must be an island," Masa asked.

"Oh, it's an island!" The sailors stormed with anger.

"Wait! When we get closer, we will know what it is," Captain Jumon said and calmed us down.

The sailors stopped talking and stared.

"Kenta, it must be an island, mustn't it?" Kyu whispered.

"I think so, too." I nodded.

Commander Roku said, "An island produces a cloud once in a while."

It looked like an island, but the shape of the island had changed.

"It was a cloud," Ichiro said, hitting the rail and crying loudly.

We worked absent-mindedly, but the island was gone. We all knew it was a cloud. Everyone cried except Iwa-san, who coolly sat on the bow of the ship.

Floating day after day, we bemoaned our destiny. Northwest winds carried us far from Japan. Sailors cried, gambled, and scooped sea water from the ship.

Commander Roku said, "We must do something."

The commander, the lieutenant, and the helmsman met. Lieutenant Nimon suggested asking god how far we were from Japan. After we were told about it, the sailors came up to god's altar and bowed deeply. I was ordered to bring the measuring box, four-fifths filled with rice. Then Captain Jumon cut five pieces of paper and wrote "two hundred miles," "one hundred miles," "eighty miles," "fifty miles," and "thirty miles." He folded them and put them inside of the measuring box. While Captain Jumon was praying, the sailors prayed to their own gods.

After prayers, the captain picked a paper from the box. "Eighty miles," he said.

"Only eighty miles." The sailors cheered.

The lieutenant said, "We must ask god when we will be home."

"If we ask two things of god," Master Chef Goro said, "God may be angry. We must be satisfied with one thing at a time."

Waves rose. Bubbles multiplied on the sea.

"A typhoon is coming!" the sailors shouted. Moreover, Master Chef Goro warned that our water would only last a few more days.

The sailors wanted to ask god when we would get home. So Captain Jumon wrote "twenty days," "thirty days," "forty days," and so on, up to one hundred. We found out we would be home in fifty days.

"It's too long."

"Only fifty days!" the sailors said, but most of them felt peace; god's message must be true.

But Iwa-san said, "The east wind is less and northwest wind is stronger. The current is the same as the wind. How could we get back to Japan?"

"Believe in god's will," Captain Jumon said.

The wind intensified. The sea and the sky turned gray. At noon, our ship swayed and strong waves came into the ship. Soon the sea water penetrated it up to three feet. We prayed and scooped the sea water. But soon some of the sailors started crying. I did not cry, but I understood their tears.

Three days had passed since the storm. The sky was blue and the wind had weakened. I worried as everyone slept. We had very little water.

Yuki, please protect us.

The northwest winds blew for three days. Our ship was forced southeast. The temperature rose. Sailors stripped half naked and talked less. Master Chef Goro ordered Kyu and me to make dried rice.

Lieutenant Nimon encouraged the sailors to scoop sea water from the ship.

My brother Ichiro cried and lay in the futon.

No rain yet.

Most wished that we had not cut the mast, but Captain Jumon calmed us down. "It was god's will, so do not complain."

Our water was less and less. I made water from steam for the first time.

I boiled the water, laid bamboo pipes in a pail and hang up the cold sea water pan.

When the steam came from the bamboo pipes, it hit the cold sea water pan, condensed, and dropped into the pipes as drinkable water.

We got a few gallons a day, but if the firewood ran out, what would we do?

Two weeks passed. There was still no rain. We distilled sea water again.

Commander Roku kept to his futon. He cried a lot. He was a very intelligent man, but he was weak in spirit. Ichiro also lay on the futon. *The men who are weak spiritually will be gone first*, I thought.

A few days later, Captain Jumon taught me the signs of a storm.

1. Increasing bubbles on the sea.
2. The wind is calm, but the sea is in an uproar.
3. There is a lot of flotsam.
4. Dark waves occur.
5. Sea water becomes warm.
6. The air grows warm, even in the winter. And you see the thunder, and then clouds spread in a horizontal line.
7. There is rain, although sometimes without rain.

I only drank a little water that day. We had rice, but not enough water. We were all eager for rain.

"Where are the rains?" Kyu asked.

Lieutenant Nimon and Iwa-san made firewood, cutting up leftover wood from the mast. We were ordered to carry this firewood to the cabin where no sea water penetrated. With few jobs left to do, the sailors fought. Iwa-san and Lieutenant Nimon worried.

We had no more vegetables and only a little wakame (seaweed) left. Master Chef Goro, Kyu and I picked seaweed from the sea. Ichiro and Commander Roku were still in their futons.

"I will cast overboard anyone who has a weak spirit!" Iwa-san shouted. When they heard Iwa-san's strong voice, Ichiro and Commander Roku got up from the futon and came up to the deck. They looked like turtles. I giggled.

When I went to the bottom of the ship, I saw someone in the dark. Kyu was crying alone. I hugged his shoulders and cried, too.

At night, Master Chef Goro served sake. Many sailors complained, "We shouldn't have cut the mast." Then they thought about their families. Ichiro cried first and then Commander Roku. Only Iwa-san stared silently at the sea.

"We must pray for rain," Captain Jumon said. Everyone agreed. Kyu danced, clapped his hands, and sang. Everyone followed Kyu's lead. After we were tired of dancing, we slept well.

In the early morning, the rain fell. We were very happy and brought all the pots, pails, and pans onto the deck. We drank our fill of water and felt fresh again.

"Cutting the mast was god's will, so stop complaining. We will get home within fifty days," Captain Jumon said.

But is there any land? I wondered. One month had passed. I had left home. I must not doubt god's will. *I must believe in god.* But sometimes I depended more on Iwa-san.

Pacific Ocean

Two and one half months had passed since we left from Atsuta on October 10.

The *Takaramaru* drifted in the Pacific Ocean. A northwest wind blew most of the time, pushing us farther from Japan. We seldom put up the sail. If we did, we would be carried away from Japan faster.

A tiny sail was little help against the strong current. The sailors were tired of drifting on the sea, but Master Chef Goro, Kyu, and I kept working. We had to cook every day.

I often took care of my brother, Ichiro, and Commander Roku. They had been lying on the futon for several days. I cooked the rice soup especially for them. Commander Roku couldn't eat much, but Ichiro still had an appetite, so he ate Commander Roku's leftovers.

"Kenta, I will die soon," Ichiro said.

Again, I thought. "Brother, don't say that. You are only eighteen. You will live for a long time," I said.

"Young or old, when we die, we die," Ichiro said.

"Brother, you still have an appetite. As long as you can eat, you will not die," I whispered.

Commander Roku slept with his mouth open. He had three children, an old mother, and sickly wife. He must have worried about them. He must have had too much pressure. Although he was a smart man, his spirit seemed to be destroyed by worry. It affected his health. But my brother, Ichiro, was still in good shape.

"Kenta, rice soup again? Bring rice and miso," Ichiro complained.

I massaged his legs. His muscles were still strong and his skin was still fresh. I remembered my father's legs. His legs were like dried vegetables, the same as Commander Roku's.

"Brother, what do our parents think about us?" I asked.

"They must think they lost two sons," Ichiro answered.

"If they could know we are still alive here, they would be so happy. I wish I could tell them our good news," I said.

"Yeah, what is Hana doing?" Ichiro asked.

When I heard the name Hana, I stopped my hands. I remembered before the ship left Onoura, Hana stepped into the sea and shook her hands so hard. *Is that our last farewell?* Hana and I were very close. "Brother, brother," she said as she followed me. From early morning to night, she was baby-sitting. She tended the children and then rushed home.

"Brother, we must go home. We must live. We shouldn't make our parents and Hana cry," I said.

"Kenta, our parents deserve to cry because they made us become sailors," Ichiro said coolly.

"Brother, you shouldn't say such a thing," I said.

"It is very true. It serves them right. They gave us this trouble. They needed money, so we became sailors. They must cry," Ichiro said.

"Brother, we must respect our parents. They didn't want us to have such troubles. We had no other way. We had no money; therefore, we couldn't start a business. Our lots are very small, so we couldn't raise enough vegetables to sell. Sailors' sons must become sailors," I said and kept on massaging his legs.

"Do sailors' sons have no other choice? We could have become carpenters or plasterers. Don't talk big, Kenta," Ichiro said and suddenly kicked my hands. I was upset, but soon I calmed down. *He still has strength.* I felt relieved. I prayed he would remain healthy.

Commander Roku opened his eyes and said, "I need to urinate."

I picked up a urine pail. There was a huge, scary moon in the sky.

~~~~~

That night, the sailors slept soundly. Lieutenant Nimon gave us a new job. He ordered us to polish everything. The sailors were tired; they slept as soon as we ate supper. The sound of men asleep filled the cabin. I put my face on the pillow.

Masa's shouting woke me. "Fool!"

Then I heard Ichiro's voice. "Masa, please let me have a drink of water. Only one sip."

I leapt from the futon and ran to them.

"No, you can't drink the water," Masa said, hitting Ichiro's shoulder.

Ichiro fell down on the floor, his hands in prayer, and begged, "Please, I need water!"

All the sailors awoke.

"What is going on?" Captain Jumon asked.

"Ichiro tried to steal the water!" Masa shouted.

"What? Water! Ichiro?" Captain Jumon asked.

Ichiro hugged Captain Jumon's leg and begged, "Captain, please give me the water. I will die without water."

Captain Jumon shook his head and said, "Ichiro, I can't give you any water. I can't break the rule."

The sailors got angry and screamed, "What shall we do about him?"

"We must beat him!"

"Indeed. The water is our life. We must not forgive someone stealing the water."

The sailors yelled and then lashed out at Ichiro.

"That is enough. By the way, Masa, how did you find out?" the captain asked.

Masa breathed deeply. "I couldn't sleep, remembering my hometown; then I saw Ichiro got up from the futon. I pretended to sleep and watched him. Ichiro touched master chef's neck."

"Then what?" Captain Jumon asked.

"Yes, then he started to steal the water box key. He removed the key string from Master Chef Goro's neck," Masa said.

"I see, so you followed Ichiro, right?" Captain Jumon asked.

"Yes, I needed proof," Masa said.

"Terrible man!"

"Tomorrow, we make him work harder."

"No, we must punish him severely," the sailors shouted.

"Captain! I don't need to drink tomorrow and the day after tomorrow. So please give him the water instead," I said and sat on the floor and bowed deeply. I cried hard.

~ ~ ~ ~

"In two more days it will be the New Year," Captain Jumon said and looked at us. Iwa-san, Lieutenant Nimon, Master Chef Goro, and I nodded. The morning sea was calm.

"Yes, two more days," Lieutenant Nimon said.

"I want to know how to celebrate New Year," Captain Jumon said.

"What do you mean?" Lieutenant Nimon asked.

"Our ship has a New Year rule, so what shall we do this coming New Year?" Captain Jumon asked.

"Captain, I want to at least prepare the New Year dishes," Master Chef Goro said.

*(New Year is the most important holiday in Japan.)

"New Year dishes? How can you cook New Year dishes only with the rice, miso, and salt?" Captain Jumon asked and opened his eyes wide.

"Indeed, we have no black beans or enough vegetables, but we have a lot of rice. I could make something like mochi using the rice. I will put them in the soup like zouni. We still have some sake," Master Chef Goro said with a smile.

"Oh, Goro! I know you are an excellent chef. What do you think, helmsman?" Captain Jumon asked.

"Whether we are in the huge sea or at home, the New Year is the New Year. We must celebrate this day," Iwa-san answered, looking at the captain.

"Oh, indeed. Everywhere we are, a New Year is a New Year!" Captain Jumon said joyfully.

"But, captain, we don't know our future. I don't feel like celebrating the New Year," Lieutenant Nimon said, almost crying.

"Captain, our ship may not reach any land, but still we have a slim hope. I bet we will reach land," Iwa-san said with his strong voice.

"Oh, do you bet?" Captain Jumon asked.

"Yes, we may die or we may live. If we think positive, we don't have to cry. So I believe we must celebrate the New Year," Iwa-san said.

"I agree with the helmsman's opinion," said Captain Jumon.

"Yes. I will try to cook my best," Master Chef Goro said; his eyes sparkled like shining stars.

"We are going to celebrate the New Year," Captain Jumon ordered.

That night, commander Roku died. His body was like a dried vegetable.

Early Spring

On January 1, 1833, Captain Jumon changed to a silk kimono. All the sailors picked their best kimonos from their wicker suitcases and then shaved their faces.

At 4:00 am, everyone stood at the stem. The moon was like thin white paper in the west, and the east side of the sky got brighter.

I am fifteen. I felt age fifteen was very grown up. We were waiting for the sunrise. Soon sharp gold light hit my eyes; the light became larger. The New Year's sun rose.

Funadama-san, please let us go home. Please protect my mother, father, Hana, and Yuki, I prayed silently. All the sailors looked at the sun.

"Is this the last New Year's sun?" Sensuke asked with a sigh.

"It might be," Jiro said.

Captain Jumon ignored their words. He entered the dining cabin. We followed him. Captain Jumon bowed to the Shinto altar, and he opened the Buddha altar and prayed. Then he looked at us.

"Captain, Happy New Year. You took care of us last year. We appreciate it. Please take care of us this year, too," Lieutenant Nimon said and bowed. The sailors followed and said, "Happy New Year, captain."

"Hmm ... today is the New Year. We have been away from Japan almost three months. I never thought I would have a New Year in this ocean," Captain Jumon continued. "We don't know what will happen tomorrow. But even if we had stayed on land, we might have had an accident and died. God made both land and sea. So even though we are on the ocean, we may have good fortune. A ship could come rescue us and take us home, or we may find a river of pure water on a beautiful island full of flowers."

"That is right! We will have good fortune tomorrow," Kyu said, which made some sailors' faces brighter.

"Oh, Kyu, you are right. We will keep up the positive thinking. Commander Roku worried too much and shortened his life. We had better think positively. Negative feelings affect our health. As long as we keep our minds strong and happy, we will not die easily. We are still surviving. It is a miracle. We had a terrible storm, but we worked together and scooped the sea water so our ship didn't sink. In the spring, the east wind will blow. Then we will go back to Japan," the captain said.

I agreed with the captain's words. Not only did people in wrecked ships die, but people on land died, too.

In spring, the east wind would blow. Then we would go back to Japan.

"Now we are going to eat New Year's dishes, which Master Chef Goro prepared," Captain Jumon ordered.

"Oh, something wonderful will be waiting for us," Kyu said.

"But the last New Year was—" Sensuke started to nag.

"What was the last New Year? Stop complaining. Today is a Happy New Year," Iwa-san said with a strong voice.

Sensuke shut his month.

"But I understand Sensuke's feeling," Lieutenant Nimon said, looking at the table.

There was zouni soup with rice dumplings, dried fish, seaweed salad, and some sake, too.

"Oh, it looks delicious. Thank you, Goro," Captain Jumon said.

Master Chef Goro sat by the table and bowed. He didn't raise his face. His nose turned red.

"Oh, it is delicious. This dumpling is better than real mochi (sticky rice)," Kyu said out loud.

"Oh, better than mochi?" Captain Jumon's eyes moistened.

Then Jiro and Masa sobbed and said, "Oh, delicious!"

"I never ate mochi at home. This is a real treat!" Kyu said and smiled.

Then Iwa-san said, "Kyu, you have spirit."

~~~~~

After I finished my dinner, I carried the tray to my brother Ichiro.

"I am sorry, brother; it's late," I said.

Ichiro slept alone after Commander Roku passed away. At night, I slept beside him.

Ichiro didn't get up, but stared at me from head to toe.

"You have a nice kimono," Ichiro said.

"I think so," I said with a smile. Genji had given me the cloth one year ago, then my mother sewed it. She tried to complete it before the New Year.

"Yes, my mother sewed it for me," I said.

"Only you have a nice kimono," Ichiro said; his eyes became sharp.

"Only me? You have a nice kimono in your wicker suitcase, but you are sick, so ..." I said.

"Kenta, does a sick man have no New Year? Don't I need to change into a new kimono?" Ichiro asked.

"I thought you didn't feel like changing," I said.

"Why did you think so?" Ichiro demanded.

"Okay, I will bring you the kimono," I said.

"It's too late now. It might be my last New Year. You didn't care about me changing to a new kimono. You are not kind even though you are my brother," Ichiro said.

"Brother, I am sorry I made you angry at the beginning of the year," I said, trying to be humble.

Ichiro had become disturbed ever since he tried to steal the water. That night, I had begged Captain Jumon, "I don't need water tomorrow or the day after tomorrow, so please let Ichiro drink the water," but Ichiro seemed to forget this fact. He just remembered that he was found by Masa and beaten by sailors.

The next day, I tried not to drink any water.

"Stupid! If you don't drink water, you will die. Even if you don't eat, you must drink water," Master Chef Goro shouted.

"My brother stole the water. I feel guilty. I can't drink water," I said.

"Oh, I can't believe Kenta and Ichiro are brothers," Captain Jumon said.

The next day, I tried not to drink water again, but Master Chef Goro said, "If you don't drink water, I will not, either," and he handed me a cup of water. I took the water cup and drank it.

When I didn't drink water, I suffered terribly. My brother felt the same way. My throat and tongue dried out and my eyes were blurred. I wanted to steal the water myself. So I understood Ichiro's bitterness, but Ichiro seemed to hate me ever since.

The sailors said, "Kenta and Ichiro are so different. Kenta didn't drink water the whole day for his brother."

I tried to calm him down and let him sit on the futon. I retrieved his kimono from his wicker suitcase. Ichiro still complained, but he changed into the kimono. Then he looked at the tray.

"Is that all? Are these the New Year dishes? There is no namasu, no umani. No vegetables at all?" Ichiro complained.

"Brother, that is impossible. But Master Chef Goro tried the best he could," I said.

"Hmm … " Ichiro looked at me sharply. "You ate better dishes, didn't you? As I am sick, you give me such dishes. I heard Kyu's joyful noise," Ichiro said.

"Kyu pretended to make happy noises in order to make things pleasant. We ate the same dishes," I said.

"Well, I don't know if that is true or not," Ichiro said and ate a dumpling. His cheeks became wet.

"Brother, why are you crying?" I asked.

"Why? Don't you know? This is my last New Year. I will be the next to die," Ichiro said, sobbing; his shoulders trembled.

"Brother, do not die!" Tears dropped from my eyes. Even though he was mean to me, he was my only brother. When we were small, we played together. He was very good at making stilts. He made me a set. I remembered our childhood.

"Oh, if I die, everyone will be happy," Ichiro said.

"What? What are you talking about?" I asked.

"Even though I don't work, I have to drink water. If I die, you can save water," Ichiro said.

I was speechless. I just looked at his face.

~~~~~

"Iwa-san, where is our ship going?" I asked.

"I don't know," Iwa-san said.

"Why don't we spread the sail?" Kyu asked.

"The west wind blows," Iwa-san said.

"Even though the west wind blows, it's okay. If we have a sail, our ship will go somewhere faster. I am tired of drifting in this ocean," Kyu said.

"Kyu, you are right. But with the west wind, our ship will sail far away from Japan," Iwa-san said.

I agreed with Kyu. But Captain Jumon and Lieutenant Nimon believed that in the spring, the east wind would blow, and then we could go back to Japan.

But Iwa-san said, "The current flows to east, and the east wind is rare. Most of the time, the northwest wind blows. Even if we made the rudder stronger, it was impossible to go against this strong current. The wind and the current are always the same way, so if we raised the sail, we would go to the east faster."

But Captain Jumon and Lieutenant Nimon were against Iwa-san and said, "We don't even know where there is land. Even if there is, the people there might kill us. We might not be able to go back to Japan."

We all waited for spring.

"You want to go home, don't you?" Iwa-san asked; his voice became gentle. "Do you know kanji?"

"I know hiragana, but not too many kanji (an alphabet that came from China)," Kyu said.

"I will teach you," Iwa-san said.

"Really?" my eyes grew wide. I knew hiragana (an alphabet the Japanese invented), but I didn't go to school often, so I didn't know too many kanji.

"We will have to do something. If you learn one or two kanji a day, it will be beneficial," Iwa-san said.

I nodded.

Scurvy

"Is it okay?"

"How about mine? It is not purple yet."

After Commander Roku's death, many sailors lost their spirit. We felt death come closer to each of us. We talked about the commander and cried. It was not because of grief for the commander; we saw our own sad future.

Every morning, the sailors examined their gums.

On January 10, the storm came again. We realized that we had less energy. We tried to scoop the sea water, but we couldn't make much progress, especially Ichiro. This storm made Ichiro weaker. The storm brought a lot of rain. Now we had a great quantity of water to drink; it filled the water tank. But the water couldn't make Ichiro well anymore.

Before the storm, there were light spots on Ichiro's body. And after the storm, the spots became darker. Ichiro looked at these spots and cried all day. His gums and nose bled. These were the same symptom Commander Roku had.

Two days before Ichiro died, he said, "Kenta, please forgive me." His voice was low but gentle.

"Brother, why do you ask forgiveness?" I asked.

"Kenta, everything I did to you was wrong. I am different from you, Kenta. You have always been a good boy, and everyone praised you, but nobody said anything good about me ... I know you and I are very different ..." Ichiro said and gasped. Blood came from his mouth.

I wiped the blood; then I felt guilty. Every time someone complimented me, Ichiro must have felt much envy. Now I understood his feelings. I said, "Brother, I am sorry. I was the bad one." I wiped his sweat from his forehead.

"No, I hated you sometimes. I like Yuki, too ... Kenta, I don't want to die," Ichiro said.

"Brother, you won't die," I said.

"No, I will die soon. But I want to see my parents one more time," Ichiro said. Tears dropped from his eyes. "But I am still happy, because you will be beside me when I die. My spirit will protect you. I promise."

"Brother!" I shouted.

"Kenta, please relax. You will surely go home. When you get home, please give my hair to my parents," Ichiro said and then sobbed.

On January 20, my brother, Ichiro, clutched at his chest and died.

~~~~~

"Captain, when we die, where do we go?" Masa asked.

"Hmm ... the monk said paradise or hell," Captain Jumon answered.

"Only paradise or hell? Is there somewhere else?" Masa asked.

"Why do you ask such a strange question?" Captain Jumon asked.

"Because I don't think I could go to paradise, but I don't want to go to hell, so I want to know if there is something else in between," Masa said.

"Masa, you must go to hell. You always fight and are mean," Jiro said.

"Oh, Masa, when Ichiro tried to steal the key from the master chef, you watched him, right?" Kazuo asked.

"Oh, I saw it," Masa said.

"I don't like it. If you had called to Ichiro when he tried to steal, he might have stopped," Kazuo said.

"Yeah, Masa's way was mean. Just before Ichiro tried to drink the water, you caught him. You should have let him drink. You are heartless," the sailors shouted. They blamed Masa.

"Masa, Ichiro must have a grudge against you. You will be cursed," Tai said.

Masa's face paled, and he shouted, "Hey! Tai, you hit Ichiro hard."

"No, Shiro and Sensuke hit Ichiro. I just watched it," Tai said.

"Stop it!" Captain Jumon shouted.

But the next moment, Masa gripped Tai's neck and said, "I will kill you!"

Then, Iwa-san stood, grabbed Masa by the neck of his kimono, and pulled his head back.

"Who is this?" Masa yelled.

"It's me. You must not act like beasts. Our death is near. You must live like human beings until then," Iwa-san said.

No one could speak against Iwa-san. Captain Jumon was too gentle, Lieutenant Nimon was subject to mood swings, but Iwa-san was reliable. Iwa-san let Masa sit in his original place and said, "No one could blame Masa, except one person, because everyone tortured Ichiro. The one person is Master Chef Goro."

The sailors looked at Master Chef Goro. "Even though he snored, he must have known someone stole the key from his neck, but he pretended to sleep. He wanted Ichiro to drink the water. Masa couldn't understand the master chef's deep thoughts. Masa was stupid, but all the sailors were complete idiots. No one could blame Ichiro's curse," Iwa-san said.

All the sailors dropped their heads.

Brother, you don't curse us, do you? You said you would protect me.

~ ~ ~ ~ ~

On April 13, Master Chef Goro died. We were all shocked. He was like our mother; he took care of our meals and health.

Every time I washed the rice, my tears fell into the pot. Master Chef Goro taught me how to wash the rice, how much water to pour into the rice, and how to cook it. Three days after, Shiro died. Their bodies swelled up.

There were only ten people left on our ship. Kyu and I had no spots on our bodies yet, but we all felt ourselves weaken.

"I don't wait for death," Tai said.

"Kenta and Kyu still have energy," Masa said.

"They are young. But why does the helmsman not have spots yet?" Tai asked.

Then Iwa-san entered the cabin. "Look!" Iwa-san showed his upper thigh. There was a dark spot.

"Iwa-san!" Kyu and I shouted. We all thought Iwa-san did not have scurvy.

"Helmsman. You must feel tired," Lieutenant Nimon said weakly.

"No, I am okay. If you keep your spirits high, you will overcome your disease," Iwa-san said.

"How?" Lieutenant Nimon asked.

"First of all, spirit," Iwa-san said.

"How about second?" Lieutenant Nimon asked.

"Spirit," said Iwa-san.

"How about third?" Lieutenant Nimon asked.

"Spirit," Iwa-san repeated.

"Oh ... we will not survive," Masa said and placed his cheek on the pillow and cried.

"Don't cry. Since February, small shells have been stuck on the ship. They were so tiny, but now they have become big shellfish. We can eat them," Iwa-san said.

"Oh! Is that true?" the sailors asked.

"And also seaweed has been stuck on the ship, too. Kenta and Kyu, you tie a rope to your waists and pick them with a bamboo colander. Because of the lack of vegetables, we have these spots on our bodies. Seaweed may be the vegetable of the sea," Iwa-san said.

Everyone ate the shellfish and the seaweed. They were good treats. Iwa-san's dark spot became lighter the next day. If we took poison, we would get sick, but if we ate nutritious food, we would be healthy. I felt stronger that morning.

"Fish! Fish!" Kyu shouted at the deck,

"What? Fish?" Iwa-san asked and picked up three fishing poles; he ran to the deck.

We caught twenty or thirty bonitos. Iwa-san made sashimi. We ate without talking. That was the most delicious sashimi ever.

"Bonito is an interesting fish. They swim following a shark," Captain Jumon said.

"Oh, shark?" Kyu asked.

"Yes, when bonitos try to catch the sardines, the shark steals the sardines. But the shark will protect the bonitos when the enemies try to attack them. Maybe these bonitos thought our ship was a shark and they followed us," Captain Jumon said.

Iwa-san, Kyu, and I cooked and dried the leftover bonitos. But that night, Tai died. Bonitos, shellfish, and seaweed couldn't give him energy anymore, because he was too sick.

On October 24, Captain Jumon dismissed his spirit.

"Get along well ..." were his last words.

Masa and Kazuo fought and fell into the sea and were gone. Then Sensuke and Jiro died a few days later.

Now only Iwa-san, Lieutenant Nimon, Kyu, and I remained alive.

Who will be next? I felt chilled. Maybe me or Kyu? If Kyu died, I would feel like I lost half of my body. If Iwa-san died, we would lose the sun from the sky. If he died, how could Kyu and I survive?

SEAGULL

We had written all the gods' names and prayed, but the sailors died one after another.

"Kyu, we may have forgotten to write a god who has more power and deep love," I said.

"Kenta, you really think so?" Kyu asked.

"Well, I have never seen the gods," I said.

"Kenta, I remember. If a god is here, he must have saved us," Kyu said.

"Yes, we gave the offering to the Shinto temple. We thought the gods would protect us if we gave. Because we paid, the gods must help us," Kyu said.

"Yeah! The gods must protect humans," I said.

"Oh, we believe that gods will take care of us so we bow and respect them. But if the gods don't help us, why should we respect them?" asked Kyu.

"Hmm ..." I nodded. "There are no gods or Buddha," I said. I felt empty while I watched Lieutenant Nimon, who bled from his mouth.

December came a second time since we left Onoura. Last December it was warm, but there was snow once in a while.

"Seagulls!" Iwa-san shouted.

"Kenta, Kyu, look! Seagulls! Lieutenant, seagulls are flying. That means land is closer," Iwa-san said.

Kyu and I hugged Iwa-san's shoulders and asked, "Have we really survived?"

"Yeah, seagulls mean a shore is near," Iwa-san said. He cried passionately. We all huddled and looked far away, but we couldn't clearly see the horizon and the sky.

"There are surely gods and Buddha," Kyu said.

The next morning, Kyu and I woke up and we went to the deck. Iwa-san was already there. "Good morning, Iwa-san," we said. He pointed with his right finger. There was no more snow, and we could see the horizon clearly; then I saw the white shining mountain. The morning sun glittered. I gazed at the white island.

"Kyu, it is winter. So there is the snow in the mountains. We can see the highest parts of land first. If we get closer, we will see the foothills and houses," Iwa-san explained.

"Is that an island? At last. There are people, fresh water, and land!" I said. Tears fell from my eyes.

Huge tears dropped from Kyu's eyes. The wind blew us toward the island. We would reach the island in three days. Our journey took one year and two months.

What kind of people would live on the land?

"Iwa-san, do you think they will eat us?" Kyu asked.

"Hmm …" Iwa-san's eyes became darker. We didn't know who lived there. But I was tired of drifting on the sea. Slowly, Iwa-san hugged Kyu and me. His warm arms encouraged me.

That night, Lieutenant Nimon died. Before he died, he said, "Helmsman, please forgive me. I shouldn't have cut the mast. It was my fault …"

Now, we were only three.

~~~~~

"Get up, Kenta, Kyu!" Iwa-san shouted.

I woke up. I followed Iwa-san.

"Lower the anchor," Iwa-san ordered.

"Anchor?" I asked.

Iwa-san pointed out the island. Huge waves swirled.

"Ei!" we dropped the anchor, but before it reached the sea bottom, our ship crashed into a sunken rock. We fell down on the deck, and then the ship started to list.

"Jump into the sea, and swim toward the island," Iwa-san said.

Iwa-san, Kyu and I dived. I felt the waves draw me to the bottom of the sea. I couldn't breathe, but the next moment, my head rose above the water. The giant waves hit my back. *A craggy place!* I felt scared; my body sank into the waves. I hugged the rock, but the waves pushed me away into the sea. Gradually I was getting closer to the island.

I grabbed a large rock. I climbed onto it. I was bruised and cut everywhere. I felt as if I were dreaming. I was deathly tired. I lay on the huge, flat rock. I slept.

~ ~ ~ ~ ~

"Kenta! Kenta!" someone was calling my name. *Is it a dream?*
"Kenta! Wake up!"
I opened my eyes. I saw Iwa-san's big eyes. "Iwa-san, is Kyu okay?" I asked.
"I am not sure," Iwa-san said.
It was in the afternoon. The wind had stopped, and the sun shone softly. The temperature was higher than in Onoura, my hometown. We were on the huge rock, and we could see the shore about half a mile away. Soon the people on the shore noticed us when we waved our hands.
"Oh, canoes!" Iwa-san said.
Two long canoes drew near us.
"Where is Kyu?" Iwa-san asked.
"Kyu! Kyu!" I shouted, but there was no answer.
"I hope Kyu didn't hit the rocks," Iwa-san said.
"If Kyu died, what will I do?" I asked and clung to Iwa-san, almost crying.
There were too many rocks and huge waves. Even though Kyu was an excellent swimmer, it was hard to swim with such angry waves.
"Oh! The island people have spears and axes," Iwa-san said.
"Are they going to kill us?" I asked, trembling.
"We must accept death with resignation. It's no use kicking and screaming now, Kenta. We must keep honor as Japanese. Don't forget," Iwa-san's eyes became dark, but he spoke with a strong voice.
The canoes stopped about twenty feet away. An old man raised two fingers.
Iwa-san thought a moment, and then he raised three fingers. They spoke. We couldn't understand their language.
"What is happening?" I asked.
"I don't know, but they may be asking how many, so I answered three," Iwa-san said and stared at them. Then the man raised one finger. Iwa-san nodded, and he pointed at the sea. Soon the canoes went back. The seagulls danced around and followed the canoes.

"Oh! Won't they help us?" I asked.

"They must be suspicious. They may think we must have more fellows," Iwa-san said.

"How do you know, Iwa-san?" I asked.

"Everyone is afraid of people they have never seen before," Iwa-san said.

"Will we be killed?" I asked.

"No, they will not kill us," Iwa-san said and sat on the rock.

"How do you know?" I asked.

"If they were going to kill us, they would have done so," Iwa-san said.

I was relieved. I looked at the sky, which was like turquoise. The sea was also blue, and we could see all the way to the bottom.

Thirty minutes later, the two canoes returned. We saw Kyu lying on one of the canoes.

"Kyu! Kyu!" Iwa-san and I shouted.

Several young men jumped on the rock from the canoe. Then they ran toward us. One of the men poked Iwa-san's shoulder with a spear. He stood up. They pushed us with the spear into the canoe. I observed each man. Their dark, bearded faces were somewhat similar to Japanese faces. Their heights were almost the same as ours. Soon we reached the shore. There were low mountains and about twenty big houses. The mountains and the beach were about half a mile apart. Children ran around the beach. When I saw the children, I felt relaxed. I smelled the pine trees. *Just like Japanese pine trees.*

Part 2 (1833-1834)

CAPE FLATTERY

The house was like a big rectangle box; only one entrance opened toward the sea. There were no lights or windows.

We were forced to enter the dark house from the bright outside sun. I couldn't see anything at first. I just smelled fish and smoke. The warm air comforted my almost naked skin. They took our kimonos and underwear. It took a while to see inside the house. Iwa-san and I sat in the center of the house, and men, women, and children surrounded us. This huge house was only one room, and there was a dirt floor. Kyu was laid on the floor, but soon he woke up.

"I am thirsty!" Kyu shouted. He rubbed his throat and opened his mouth. He showed his tongue, joined his hands, and bowed. He pretended to drink water. An older man nodded and said something. Soon someone brought a big water pitcher and wooden bowls.

"Thank you!" Kyu said and raised the bowl, bowed again, and drank it. Iwa-san and I drank quietly.

"Good!" Iwa-san said. We wet our throats. The water was pure. They were watching us drink it. Then Kyu pushed his stomach and pretended to chew food. The older man ordered something. Soon a man brought several boiled potatoes and smoked salmon on a tray.

"Thank you," Kyu said and held the smoked salmon and ate it. His eyes opened wide and he ate one after another. We had never eaten potatoes before; they were sweet and tasty. We had been eating rice for fourteen months, so the potatoes and smoked salmon were delicious.

After we finished eating, the oldest man asked something.

"What did he say?" Kyu asked.

"Maybe he asked where we came from," Iwa-san guessed. "Japan, Japan," Iwa-san repeated, and he wrote "Japan" in Japanese.

One of them imitated and said, "Japan."

"I am Iwa," Iwa-san said and pointed his finger at his chest. "And he is Kyu," Iwa-san said and pointed at Kyu. "He is Kenta," Iwa-san said and put on his hand on my shoulder.

The land we had reached after fourteen long months was the west side of North America, Cape Flattery. (Now it is a part of Washington State.) There was Vancouver in Canada, which was the north. The people who surrounded us were called the Cape Indians. We were caught as their slaves. I didn't even know the word *slave*; I learned it later. They believed that anything that came into their land was their property: the seaweed and wood that the waves washed up, and humans as well. We are counted as things.

Most of the slaves were gained as spoils of war. Once in a while, they went to Vancouver and bought slaves, but they had to exchange them for ten or twenty valuable blankets. But now they had three slaves without either war or exchanging blankets. Happiness filled this house. They kept on asking questions, one after another, but we couldn't understand their language. Neighbors came to see their luck, as if saying, "Why didn't even one of them come to our shore?" They sighed.

All the men had long hair tied in the back. Women had earrings and bracelets and wore long clothes. Their figures were similar to Japanese women. Children came to me and touched my back. "Kenta, Kenta," they said, laughing.

I felt relieved. When we were thirsty, they gave us water, and when we were hungry, they gave us food. It was not too bad.

But I didn't understand about being a slave. Later I found out many things. When a chief dies, his most favorite slave was killed and buried with him. Also when the chief invited many guests over and had a party, he cut off a slave's head in order to show off his property. "I don't mind if I lose one or two slaves. I have a lot."

The people tired of asking us questions. Then they let us sleep. They knew we were tired. They didn't want us to be sick, as we were their slaves.

I lay on a simple bed. I looked around. It was a huge house, but many wood cases, baskets, and boxes divided the space. The blankets and clothes were in the boxes, and food was in baskets hanging from the ceiling. Many couples lived in this house. The chief gave us jackets made from cedar bark.

~ ~ ~ ~ ~

Two weeks passed. In a few more days it would be a new year. We became healthy again. The Cape Indians called us Kenta, Kyu, and Iwa. They knew our names at once, but it was hard for us to remember their names. A friendly man was Dou-Dark-Teal (young bird), and a man who was extremely mean was called Ah-Dank (fire). But they were only nicknames. The Cape Indians had no names. They only had a line of descent.

When Kyu and I picked up the firewood, we saw our ship, the *Takaramaru*, on the beach. After they saved us, the Indians pulled in the ship using ropes made of seaweed and cedar roots. They waited for a high tide and brought the ship to the beach.

When they saw the dead bodies, they were surprised, but they took care of the bodies carefully. Captain Jumon, Lieutenant Nimon, Master Chef Goro, Ichiro, and Sensuke were buried in the woods. (The other bodies were buried at sea a long time ago.)

The Cape Indians took everything in the ship. The rice, ship cabinets, kimonos, an ink stone case, ship logs, and wicker suitcases were all theirs. They gave us crude jackets and salmon-skin shoes instead. Usually we walked barefoot, but when we picked up the water from the spring, we used the salmon-skin shoes. We had to walk a few miles to get it, but we loved this distance. We filled deer-skin bags with water. Iwa-san made a carrying pole, which helped me carry the water. Friendly deer drank water, too. Bears lived in the mountains, but they must have been hibernating.

Every time we passed the burial grounds, we stopped and prayed.

"Brother, you protect us. Thank you," I murmured.

"Funadama-san protects us, too," Kyu said, smiling.

We enjoyed walking in the mountains. From morning to night, we became tense, because Ah-Dank whipped us without any reason. Every time he whipped me, I felt as if I were a cow or a horse. Other Indians were kinder. I couldn't believe Ah-Dank and the chief were brothers. We called Ah-Dank *mamushi* (viper).

"Kyu, do we have to live here the rest of our lives?" I asked.

"Well, we have no big ship. Even if we had a ship, we have no guarantee we can go back to Japan. Kenta, one of us can marry the chief's daughter," Kyu said.

"Hmm …"

"I like Piko. I want to marry her," Kyu said as if he were dreaming.

Piko was the chief's daughter. The Cape Indians sometimes whipped the slaves, but there was no discrimination between the slaves and the Indians. They went fishing and gathered firewood together. The slaves could marry the Indians, and the chief could marry the slaves. They each had one wife or one husband, except the chief. The chief had three wives in the house. If a husband beat his wife too much, sometimes the wife left with her children, and she could marry someone else.

I thought of Yuki. She would be sixteen this year. *Yuki, don't marry anyone. Yuki! I will surely get home! But how?*

WHIP

It was midnight. People woke up and lanterns came on. Men were going to catch whales. Dou-Dark-Teal called, "Iwa! Iwa!" but he still slept. "Iwa! Iwa!" he called Iwa-san again. Then Ah-Dank came and beat Iwa-san's shoulder with a whip. Iwa-san woke up. Ah-Dank's eyes became sharp, and he beat Iwa-san again.

"Why do you beat me?" Iwa-san glared at him. His voice was big, like a man who trained as the helmsman. Ah-Dank's mouth curved and he hit Iwa-san's shoulder a third time.

"You, pig!" Iwa-san shouted, and he stood up and glared at Ah-Dank.

Dou-Dark-Teal stood between Iwa-san and Ah-Dank and asked, "Why do you beat him?"

"Iwa is lazy!" Ah-Dank said and tried to beat Dou-Dark-Teal.

Then the chief appeared and said something in a low voice. He patted Ah-Dank's shoulder. They said something to each other, but Ah-Dank shook his head and his whip and then left.

The chief's wife brought a small pot and spread oil on Iwa-san's shoulders. The Cape Indian women's fingers were powerful because of their hard-working habits.

Soon all the men went whale catching. The chief left, too. After the men left, the women and children went back to their beds. Iwa-san lay on the mat.

"Iwa-san, you hurt, don't you?" I asked.

"Mamushi is crazy!" Kyu cursed.

Every day Kyu and I were beaten by Ah-Dank (Mamushi). Other Indians told us things by gesture, but Ah-Dank whipped us a few times a day—but we never got welts. But today, Ah-Dank hit Iwa-san terribly. Maybe because Iwa-san spoke against him.

"Can you sleep, Iwa-san?" I asked, patting his shoulder.

"Don't worry, Kenta," Iwa-san said and laughed slightly. "I want to drink sake."

"Why don't they have any sake?" asked Kyu.

"Yes, Iwa-san likes sake. It's a shame," I said. The Cape Indians had no sake.

"Kenta, Kyu," Iwa-san said and got up, looking at us. His face was very serious, and his eyes became sharp like knives.

"What?" Kyu and I asked.

"I will escape!" said Iwa-san.

"How, Iwa-san?" I asked.

"Not right now. But I will escape somehow," Iwa-san said.

"Only you?" I asked.

"It's up to you," said Iwa-san.

"Of course, Iwa-san. Right, Kenta?" Kyu asked.

"Yes, we are always with you, Iwa-san. Whether we live or die," I said.

"Oh, okay. I can't stand to see Mamushi's face. I want to kill him. It would be easy to kill him, but the rest would be too much trouble after that. So I have to run away from here." Iwa-san continued, "I am thinking about writing a letter."

Once in a while, canoes came from Vancouver. They brought the blankets, flour, and sugar. Iwa-san was going to give the letter to one of the canoes' men. Even though they couldn't read Japanese, someone would understand his letter was asking for help.

But how could he write? The chief took our ink stone case, which had the writing brushes and papers. We had never seen the chief write letters. No one wrote anything in this house. They painted a strange bird, which was called Thunder Bird, on the doors, posts, and walls. The Thunder Bird had huge wings that could cover the sky; then when the bird moved its wings, thunder occurred. Every time the thunder struck, all the men went to the mountains. They also believed that a giant who ate whales lived in the mountains. The giant put on a big bird head and large wings, and he also hung sparkling fish on his hip. Every time the thunder struck, the sparkling fish fell down from his hip. If Indians could find even the fish bones, they would be expert whale fishermen. The Thunder Bird was like the Cape Indians' hero.

"Kenta, Kyu, all the men went to catch a whale. They won't come back until tomorrow afternoon," Iwa-san said. "We must take the writing brush and the ink."

"But the women are still watching," I said with awe.

"Hmm … Kyu and Kenta, you must do something to attract their attention tomorrow. When everyone goes outside, I will go inside and take the ink stone case. I don't think it is stealing. They stole ours. I want to tell them to return it, but I can't communicate with them," said Iwa-san.

"Okay. Iwa-san, but what shall I do?" I asked.

We thought and thought. Then I got an idea. "Ah, Iwa-san, I was good at walking on stilts," I said.

"That is a good one," Kyu said.

"I can make the stilts easily. So you both jump around with the stilts. Everyone will come out and look," Iwa-san said, smiling.

We were excited and couldn't wait until the morning came. At last, the sun rose.

Without men, the house was peaceful. The women chattered and made baskets.

The children ran in and out noisily. Every time the men left to fish, the women and children had a sense of freedom, because sometimes husbands shouted at their wives and slapped their cheeks.

Kyu and I made stilts. Iwa-san was making a water pail. Before lunch, we rode the stilts and walked into the house. Everyone was surprised; then we went out. All the children and women followed us.

I looked at Iwa-san. He stood up and went inside the house.

Iwa-san hid the papers, brush, and the ink in my basket on the bed. My bed was the third bunk bed. Today I lay on Iwa-san's first bunk bed, and Iwa-san used my bed in order to write a letter.

He wrote, *On October 10, 1832, the* Takaramaru *left Japan with fourteen sailors. Eleven out of fourteen died. Iwa, Kyu, and Kenta survived. After the storm, we floated on the sea for one year and two months. Now we have been captured as slaves. If someone reads this letter, please help us. Our lives are in danger. We want to go back to Japan. Please help us as soon as possible.*

January 5, 1834

Iwa

~ ~ ~ ~ ~

Cold wind blew, and the clouds covered the sun. We made ropes with the Indians at the beach.

The Cape Indians made many kinds of ropes. They used the seaweed or the cedar bark. Now we made ropes with the muscle of a whale. We divided the dead whale muscle into fibers like linen. Then we twisted them in our hands on our thighs. Then the fibers became threads. We rolled the threads and made ropes that needed patience and time, but these ropes were better quality than the ropes that white people made. Every time the fiber rubbed my thigh, blood came oozing out.

"Ah, I am tired," Kyu said.

"Me, too." I nodded.

Iwa-san looked at the lead-colored sea. It was on January 15. I thought there was New Year all over the world, but the Cape Indian counted only two seasons. The winter solstice was the beginning of the year, and the summer solstice was another beginning of the year. Nobody knew their age. After two years, the parents couldn't count the child's age. December was California-Gray-Whale-Coming Month and January was Month of Whale Bearing Child. They had no letters or numbers.

"Are there any gods here?" I asked

"I don't think there is any place without gods," Kyu answered.

"Hmm, but I don't see any altars here," I said.

"Oh, look!" Kyu said.

We saw a big canoe. It appeared and came closer to the beach. Then we heard drums. The Cape Indians pointed to the canoe and said something. Gradually, the adults and children ran and stood at the beach.

"What! War?" Kyu asked.

"Only one or two canoes. It must not be war," Iwa-san said. He kept on working and laughed.

Then another canoe came and another.

"The canoes keep on coming, Iwa-san," I said.

All of a sudden, Ah-Dank shouted and ran toward the house. Then the men carried ropes and strings and everyone followed Ah-Dank. Soon the house door was shut.

"Should we run away?" Kyu asked; his face paled.

We were the only three left on the beach.

Iwa-san stopped working and looked around. Only the chief's family went into the house, but other people came and smiled and looked at the canoes. "It's not war or a fight," Iwa-san said and worked.

"Hmm …" Kyu looked at the canoes with uneasy eyes.

There were five canoes and seven or eight men were in each canoe.

"They have no bows and arrows or axes," Iwa-san said, smiling.

I felt relieved. Seagulls cried and danced on the five canoes.

Men sang with a drum.

"Oh, it's like a festival," Kyu said, clapping his hands.

"Hmm … the chance has come," said Iwa-san. He wrapped the letter with cedar bark and tightened it with a string and hid it in his robe. He touched his chest with his hand.

The canoes had stopped. Then the men became quiet. In a moment, the beach became silent.

One young man with beautiful muscles stood and spoke. I couldn't understand everything that he said, but I guessed, "Ladies and gentlemen. I live in the next village. I come to propose marriage to beautiful Piko. I will pay many blankets. Please let me marry Piko."

When his speech had finished, the men brought the blankets from the canoe. They left the canoes and marched onto the beach. An older man who seemed to be a fortune-teller with a red, blue, and yellow robe walked first. His face was painted red, and bundled eagle feathers were on his head. He held a cane, and all the men followed him.

"Lot of blankets," Kyu said and tilted his head.

The Cape Indians gave us old blankets. We washed them and used them for sleep at night and also as clothing during the day. The blanket was a very valuable thing for the Indians.

The men placed many blankets in front of the chief's door. The door was closed tight. The men went back to the canoes and brought more blankets. Still nobody opened the door.

Then the men started singing again.

"He is a good man.

He is the best whale catcher.

He rows the canoes the fastest.

He could afford to give fifty blankets to you.

He is rich.

He is a good man."

They danced and sang enthusiastically. They marched toward us. The fortune-teller stopped walking and looked at us. He must have felt we were not Indians. A few days ago, we tied our hair back and put on cedar bark robes, but still our faces were different from the Indians. The men stopped dancing and surrounded us. The fortune-teller said something. Then one man said, "Chief." Someone told him that we were slaves of the chief. He came closer and gave us a warm smile.

"Where did you come from?" asked the fortune-teller.

"Japan," I answered.

"Japan," the fortune-teller repeated.

Then they said, "Japan, Japan."

The fortune-teller tried to smell us and touched our hands and feet.

"Slaves," he murmured. The fortune-teller said something with a loud voice. Then the men formed a line again, dancing and singing. The line moved away, but the fortune-teller stood still and asked us many questions.

Iwa-san quickly pulled the letter from his chest and put it on the sand. The fortune-teller was puzzled. Iwa-san bowed deeply and put his hands together. The fortune-teller tried to open the letter.

"Not now!" Iwa-san said and waved his hand and showed his whip scars. Kyu and I bowed and put hands together many times. Iwa-san pretended to put the letter in his bosom. The fortune-teller nodded, and he put his finger on his lips. We put our fingers on our lips, too.

Do not tell anyone! we cried inwardly.

The fortune-teller stood up. Iwa-san breathed a sigh of relief. I felt my body sweat. Kyu gazed blankly at the fortune-teller's back. We had done the best we could.

When the fortune-teller reached the line, the men stopped singing. Then the man who proposed marriage started to speak. "Dear pretty Piko, I have never missed catching a whale. Also, I can row a canoe the fastest. If you don't believe it, I could race with your best canoe man. You can't find a better man than me."

Other men clapped their hands.

The man continued talking. "Dear Piko, you better marry me. You will be the happiest wife. If you need more blankets, I will bring them tomorrow. Please think of me. You can't find another wonderful man like me." Then they sang and danced again.

"Iwa-san, even if someone gets the letter, nobody can read it," I said.

"It's okay. The letter was proof that some foreigners live here as slaves," said Iwa-san.

"But if nobody can read it, they won't understand it," Kyu said.

"It doesn't matter. Whoever received the letter will tell someone else, 'Some foreigners arrived in that land and gave me a letter. It means help! I saw their scars from the whip. It was pitiful,'" Iwa-san said and kept on working.

"Oh, I see. Even though they can't read it, someone will tell someone else. But if the chief or Mamushi hear, they will kill us," Kyu said with low voice.

"If so, we will run away to the mountains," Iwa-san said.

"Yeah! But we may meet scary people," said Kyu.

"Indeed!" I said.

Then we all became silent.

The men stopped dancing and singing. But nobody came out from the house. That meant they didn't want to let Piko marry for only fifty blankets. The men gave up and returned to the canoe with the blankets. They followed the fortune-teller and went back to the canoes.

We all watched the canoes leaving.

"Lazy!" We heard a loud voice,

"Oh, Mamushi!" Kyu shouted.

We worked again, but it was too late. The whip hit Kyu's back and then Iwa-san's shoulder. Iwa-san bit his lip tight. Mamushi didn't hit me and then left.

They must have pain. I felt sorry for them.

"Ahh, we have to eat leftovers from the children's meal. When we stopped working, Mamushi whipped us. We are like cows or horses," Kyu complained.

I looked at the early spring sea. It was cloudy between the sea and the sky.

~~~~~

The sky was blue. The sun shone onto the mountain and the sea. Kyu and I gathered the seaweed at the beach with the children. The odor of herring was still on the beach. A lot of dried herring laid on every roof.

"Kenta, Kenta ..." the children always followed me. A girl whose name was Shu-Fove reminded me of my sister, Hana; I called her Hana.

All the children were naked. Kyu and I just wrapped our hips with a cloth.

For the past few days, the sea had been rough. The huge waves carried a lot of seaweed. Some of it was thin and some like snakes. When the children saw the huge pieces of seaweed, they were excited. They threw small stones at the seaweed as if it were a whale and the small stones were like harpoons. Everyone's face became red, and they threw the stones very seriously. Even four- or five-year-old children's eyes sparkled.

"Kenta, these children are different from Japanese children," Kyu said.

"Indeed," I replied. We had never played like that. The Indians threw stones as if the seaweed were like a real whale. Every time a stone hit the seaweed, they made joyful noises. They didn't stop throwing the stones until the seaweed became completely broken up.

"It's weird," Kyu said.

"Yes, but catching whales is a very important thing here, and the best whale catcher will be highly respected," I said.

"It's true, but I don't feel good about it. They don't have to throw the stones so much. I feel as if blood will come from the seaweed," Kyu said, curling his lips.

All the Indians, men, women, boys, and girls became frantic. The whale catching was the only fulfillment in their lives.

"The other children practiced whale catching," Kyu said and pointed at the sea.

There were several small canoes on the sea, and boys rowed the canoes skillfully. The Indian boys needed this kind of play from an early age in order to practice their profession.

Kyu and I carried the seaweed and placed it on the beach. Then we picked up more seaweed. Every time we worked on such a monotonous thing, we remembered our hometown and family.

"Let us take a break," Kyu remarked.

"Is Mamushi not coming?" I asked.

"No, he is fixing the house right now. But why doesn't Mamushi whip you?" asked Kyu.

"I don't know, but I am sorry. You and Iwa-san are beaten all the time," I apologized. At first, I couldn't understand why Mamushi didn't whip me. But soon I found out the reason. Every time Mamushi whipped me, the children got angry, cried, and shouted at Mamushi. So he stopped whipping me. Moreover, the chief liked me very much. He gave me special food, and even a seal fur. I felt bad every time the chief treated me as if I were special.

"Kenta, you are always welcomed. You became the fiancé of Yuki in Japan, and the Indian chief also treats you special," Kyu said.

"I am sorry, Kyu," I said.

"No, you don't have to say sorry. We are happy one of us isn't beaten. If three of us were all ill-treated, we would be more miserable," Kyu said with a smile.

We stood up and gathered the seaweed again.

When we got home, Piko's brother, Dou-Dark-Teal, wore a bird mask and practiced dancing. He would dance at Piko's wedding. Once in a while, the big bird's mouth opened and bit the children's head. The children jumped back, but they wanted to see the mouth open, so they came close to Dou-Dark-Teal. All of a sudden, the children shouted for joy. The mask's mouth opened wide, and another face appeared. The new face was red, blue, and black. It was an interesting trick.

Piko's wedding was only a few days away. A man came so many times to ask Piko to marry him. He brought sixty blankets, so at last the chief was satisfied and accepted the proposal for Piko.

At the party, it was the custom for the chief to destroy a very important thing or to kill a slave.

Is the chief going to kill us, too?

Two Masts

I was still very sleepy.

"Kenta!" Kyu said and shook my shoulders. I got up. The chief and other people were excited. Iwa-san stood by the door. Many people were outside, and then they started to run. We followed them.

"Oh, ships!" I shouted.

Each ship had two masts, and the morning wind blew on the sails. They ran quickly through the sea.

"Big ships!" Kyu said. "Where are they going?"

"They are coming here," Iwa-san said and looked at the ships.

"This beach?" asked Kyu.

"Yes!" Iwa-san said.

"If we escape to that ship, will we be safe?" Kyu asked again.

"I don't know," Iwa-san said and kept on watching the ships.

When everyone knew the ships were coming toward this beach, the chief went back home and all men and women followed him. Everyone looked cheerful.

"Iwa, Kenta, Kyu!" the chief called us. He ordered us to carry seal fur boxes. We held up these boxes and sat them in front of the house.

"It must be the merchant ships," Kyu said.

"Maybe, but they are huge ships. Are they the same size as the *Takaramaru*?" I asked.

"Hmm ... I think they are larger than the *Takaramaru*," Iwa-san said. "They have two masts. We can go back to Japan with those ships, Kenta."

"Iwa-san, is that true?" I asked; my heart was full of joy.

"Yes!" Iwa-san said, nodding.

"But we can't steal the ship," Kyu said.

"Kenta, Kyu. They must have come to save us," Iwa-san said, still looking at the small boats being lowered from the ships to the sea.

"To save us!" Kyu said; his eyes grew wide.

"My sixth-sense said that," Iwa-san said; his eyes sparkled. "The letter must have reached them."

"The letter!" I said.

~ ~ ~ ~ ~

Iwa-san, Kyu, and I sat on the sand.

The chief and a man stood nearby, and a translator spoke each language. The man was tall, with blue eyes, bronze hair, and a beard. He had a hooked-nose. I had never seen such a face before. All the men who came from the ship wore different clothes than the Cape Indians. Their sleeves were narrow, the collars were folded down, and their pants were baggy. The Cape Indians' robes had no sleeves, so I knew at once they were different from the Indians.

I found out later that the merchant ship came every three years. The man was Captain White, who worked at the Hudson Bay Company in England. The Hudson Bay Company had a monopoly on the fur trade in Canada. In 1670, King Charles II gave a special permit to eighteen noblemen who built this company. This company was a powerful force in England rather than just a company. Captain White was an American. He thought we were Chinese. His ship sailed all over the world. He was going back to Fort Vancouver in Canada and then to England. From England, some ships went to China, so he was going to send us there.

As he was also a sailor, he knew how hard it was to sail the huge sea, and now he saw that we were slaves. He wanted us to return to our home country. He tried to trade for us with blankets, tea pots, pans, flour, and sugar.

But the chief said, "They are hard-working slaves. They enjoy working here."

"I don't believe it," Captain White said and pulled the letter from his pocket.

I looked at Iwa-san. He fixed his eyes on the letter.

The captain opened the letter and showed it to Iwa-san. He pointed at the letter and pretended to write.

"You wrote this letter, didn't you?" the captain asked

We had never heard such language, but Iwa-san nodded. The translator said the Indian's words.

"Oh!" the chief and other people shouted.

Iwa-san pointed to his chest and said, "I wrote it!"

"Dr. John McLoughlin, who was called the Father of Oregon, is in charge of all of the Pacific Ocean at the Hudson Bay Company. He received it on May 24," the captain said.

"Hmm …" the chief groaned.

"Last year, we heard that there was a wrecked Chinese ship. We tried to save them, but it was winter. The wind and the waves were very strong, so we couldn't reach the wrecked ship," the captain explained.

I listened to his words carefully. His words were different from the Cape Indians'. I learned for the first time that people spoke many different languages.

"We couldn't understand what he wrote, but Dr. McLoughlin thought this letter was for help. So he ordered us to help these poor Oriental men. We gave you blankets, pots, pans, flour, sugar, butter, and even women's clothing," the captain said with a smile.

The chief listened through the translator.

"I understand, but they are extremely hard-working slaves," the chief insisted.

"Yes, Dr. McLoughlin said we must try our best. I will pay you well," the captain said.

"I can exchange Iwa and Kyu for the blankets, but not Kenta," the chief remarked.

"Why not Kenta?" the captain asked.

"I can't find a man like him. I wouldn't mind him being my son-in-law. I even forbid him being whipped," the chief said.

"Chief, I understand your special feeling toward Kenta, but his father, mother, brothers, and sisters love him, too. If you are a parent, you must understand Kenta's parents' feeling, as well," Captain White said.

"Well, I have to think about it. We have a wedding party tomorrow. So we will talk about it after the wedding," the chief said.

Piko's wedding lasted for three days. Many guests came from everywhere. There were fish, meat, and vegetables in big containers that had four wheels were carried to the guests. The neighbor women cooked these dishes.

Dou-Dark-Teal danced well.

Piko was pretty in her wedding dress. The party started in the late afternoon and ended in the early morning. We worked hard for three days. At last, Piko and her groom rode in the canoe and left. Piko's cheeks were wet and she waved to us for a long time. We all stood at the beach and watched them until they disappeared.

After the wedding, Captain White and the chief talked again.

"How about twenty blankets and three guns? You must think of Kenta's parents' feelings," the captain insisted.

"Guns!" the chief said; his eyes grew wide.

At last the chief agreed to let me go. Kyu and I held each other's hands tight and cried.

Fort Vancouver

In 1834, there was famine in Japan. The cost of rice was extremely high, and riots occurred in Osaka. Moreover, a huge fire destroyed Edo.

Republican rebels were against the government in France.

Exporting opium to China was blocked in England, and that would be the cause of a war.

I didn't know anything about these circumstances, and we were on the ship on the Columbia River in America.

"Just like a dream," I said.

"Indeed," Iwa-san said while looking at the forest.

The ship was 145 tons—not huge. Captain White and all the other sailors were very kind to us. As they were sailors, they admired us. Crossing from Japan to America was hard, even with a perfect ship, but we had floated with a broken ship. In order to survive, we had needed extremely strong wills and spirits. They understood and seemed to respect us.

"I am glad we are all together," Kyu said.

"Yes, all the Indians came to say farewell at the beach. Someone gave me dried fish and hair ribbon to tie my hair back," I said.

"Yes, but I don't want to see them again," Kyu said.

I remembered the children and Dou-Dark-Teal; he led us to the graveyard before we left. He must have watched us as we prayed.

"Brother, I must go. Good-bye." I bowed to my brother Ichiro's gravestone and to other people's gravestones as well.

"Brother, thank you for protecting me," I murmured.

The Colombia River was huge, and we saw a ship with three masts come toward our ship.

"A huge ship!" Kyu said in awe.

We had learned some Indian language, but now we didn't understand anything. We only learned *bread*, *cup*, and *water*.

But Iwa-san said, "Even though we can't understand their words, we can learn how to control the sails and tiller just by looking. You must learn those things."

I agreed with Iwa-san. Their eating manner and way of cleaning the ship was different, but I learned their ways just by observing them.

"This ship is very well made. The floor was fixed with good wood, so the sea water does not penetrate the ship," Iwa-san said and admired it.

"Oh, Mount Fuji!" Kyu shouted.

"Fuji?" Iwa-san asked and looked far away.

We saw a mountain just like Mount Fuji on the far left.

"The mountain is like Mount Fuji, but it is not," said Iwa-san.

The mountain that made us excited was 4,392 meters in height, Mount Rainier. Later, Japanese immigrants called it Tacoma Fuji.

The ship arrived at Fort Vancouver. Captain White came closer and talked to us. Then he waved to the people at the harbor. Kyu and I waved to them also. Around one hundred people stood at the harbor and waited for us.

A ramp was built to the shore. The captain held my shoulders and went first.

Funadama-san! I shut my eyes and shouted in my heart. I was scared of what kind of life was waiting for us in this strange place.

As soon as we stood on the shore, the people dashed to us. I saw some Indians' faces, but their robes were different from the Cape Indians. Some wore suits, black shirts, and pants with suspenders. The women's clothes were very strange to me. Their waists were small, and they had skirts like balloons. I felt the Cape Indians' robes were normal. They had blonde or red hair, and blue eyes. *Funadama-san!* I felt as if they were oni (Japanese monsters); I was terrified.

The captain said something loudly. The people moved out of the way, but they were still excited. They must think we were unusual Orientals. They were also informed that we sailed in the Pacific with a broken ship. They wanted to praise us.

All of a sudden, a boy about ten years old dashed to me and hugged me. His hair was black and his eyes were brown. His cheeks became red like apples. The boy said something fast. His voice was high like a broken piano. "You were great. You sailed with a broken ship on the Pacific for many months without water and food. You are a hero. I couldn't do that!"

The people agreed with his words and clapped their hands.

The boy continued, "I admire your patience and courage. I want to be like you. I will go to Japan someday. Please be friends with me."

I couldn't understand his words, but I felt kindness from his expression.

"Ronald," a woman called his name.

The boy stood tall and held his hands up to my neck. I lowered my face; then he pushed his lips to my left cheek. I was traumatized. I thought he had bit me. But of course he had not. That was the first kiss that I had received in my life. Ronald went back to the lady.

Ronald's father was the person in charge of the Hudson Bay Company. The woman who had called Ronald's name was his stepmother. Ronald's biological mother was a daughter of an Indian chief and had died a long time ago.

Ten years later, Ronald went to Japan as a stowaway aboard a whaling ship. When Ronald reached Japan, he was arrested by the Nagasaki magistrate. While he was in Nagasaki, Japan, he taught English to Japanese translators. Ronald's motivation for going to Japan was his knowledge of our experiences. Moreover, Ronald thought his biological mother was Japanese. He learned Japanese from us, and it was helpful when he was in Japan. Later, the foreign delegation, Moriyama Takichiro, who learned English from Ronald, visited me when I was in Singapore.

Ronald McDonald was the first person to introduce English to Japan.

We followed the captain. Fort Vancouver was a tiny village in a huge forest. A high, strong wooden fence surrounded this village, and there was a fort in order to prevent Indian attacks.

"Kenta, is it a jail?" Kyu whispered.

"I don't think so. The gate is open, and people are going in and out," I said, but I felt uneasy.

On the right side of the fort, there was a watch tower, and a house with two chimneys was on the left. The people on the shore still followed us. At last, we passed the fort gate. We saw a carriage leaving the gate.

"Oh, the horse is different from Japanese horses. It's very big!" Kyu said, rolling his eyes.

There were twenty houses in the fort. These houses were made from logs. After we passed the gate, we saw a big two-story house with white paint.

"Kyu! The windows are taller than they are broad," I shouted.

"Yes, Japanese windows are long sideways, with paper screens. But these windows shine with the sun light. What are they?" Kyu asked.

"It must be glass," Iwa-san answered.

"Oh, glass! They are too bright," Kyu said.

Captain White smiled and led us inside the house. The largest house inside the fort was Dr. John McLoughlin's house. It had a cedar roof.

A man who stood by the door welcomed us. His eyes and eyebrows were close together, and his upper lip was long. The man said something with a loud voice, and he held Iwa-san's hand tightly, and then Kyu's hand and mine. Then he hugged our shoulders. I felt he was a man we could depend on.

The floor was polished wood, but nobody took off their shoes. We passed by a huge dining table with a white tablecloth and entered another room. They let us sit on the couch, and Dr. McLoughlin and the captain sat on the armchairs. Then they prayed.

It is not meal time yet, so why do they pray? I was puzzled. I saw sailors pray before they ate and slept on the ship. They just clasped their hands to their chest. But now they were praying with loud voices.

On the ship there were no Shinto or Buddhist altars. There was no Funadama-san. I felt they were impious.

After Dr. McLoughlin's long prayer, we were taken outside the house. A very talkative Indian servant took us to a river. The Indian gestured to us to remove our robes and then pointed out the river.

"Hmm ... we must wash our body in the river," Kyu said.

We took off our robes and went in the river. The Indian gave us a bar of hand soap and taught us how to use it.

"I am Da-Ka," the Indian said.

Da-Ka meant "moon." This talkative Indian man's face was round as a moon.

"Da-Ka," Kyu said with a smile.

We had heard Indian words and could understand the meaning, so we felt as if we were at home.

"Kyu, Iwa, and Kenta," Kyu introduced us.

When we came out of the river, he gave us big towels. We thought they were our new robes, so we tried to figure out how to wear them.

"Oh, no!" Da-Ka laughed. He handed out black shirts from a basket.

"These are underwear," Da-Ka said. We put them on. Then Da-Ka gave us baggy pants.

Iwa-san was tall, so the pants fit him, but my pants were too long and I walked trailing the pants behind me. Kyu and I laughed, but we also felt like crying when we saw Iwa-san. He did not look Japanese anymore.

If we are in foreign country, we must follow their customs, I almost said, but I felt as if Japan were far away; I shut my mouth.

We went back to Dr. McLoughlin's house again. I felt my sleeves were tight, and I was also uncomfortable with my baggy pants. Moreover, the shoes hurt my feet so bad, I took them off and held them in my hands.

When Dr. McLoughlin saw us, he said something. He must have said, "They fit well."

We bowed deeply.

"Thank you for your kindness," Iwa-san said in Japanese.

Dr. McLoughlin nodded. Then he asked us, "How old are you?"

But of course we couldn't understand.

He pointed one finger and said, "One." Then he held up two fingers then three fingers. "Four, five, six ..." he pointed to his fingers. He repeated, "One, two, three ... "

We strained our ears to hear.

"One is a number," I said.

Dr. McLoughlin drew a big circle and drew ten small circles in the big circle. Then he said, "How old are you?" He drew a big circle and four small circles outside the big circle.

"Oh, they must be asking our age," I said and I drew two more small circles outside the big circle.

"Oh, you are sixteen!" Dr. McLoughlin shouted. "How old are you?" he asked Kyu.

Kyu added one small circle.

"Oh, seventeen," Dr. McLoughlin said and asked Iwa-san.

Iwa-san drew three big circles.

"Oh, thirty!" the captain and Dr. McLoughlin said and nodded.

Then Dr. McLoughlin asked us to draw our ship. We didn't understand at first, but he drew a ship with two masts and then he drew a ship without the mast.

"Maybe he wants me to draw the *Takaramaru*," Iwa-san said.

"It must be," I agreed.

Iwa-san drew the mast and sails of the *Takaramaru*. He drew a picture of the rice bags. His drawing explained our lives as if it were in a picture book. Dr. McLoughlin and the captain were amazed at Iwa-san's drawing. Iwa-san picked up another new paper and he put the *Takaramaru* on the calm waves. Then he drew the high waves like mountains, and with thunder. He indicated the strong wind by black lines. Then he drew on the next paper that we threw away some rice bags to make the ship lighter and then cut the mast. Dr. McLoughlin and the captain held their breath.

Iwa-san kept on drawing. One man died and then two ... our ship hit the rocks and then we became the Indians' slaves. He also drew Ah-Dank whipping us. Dr. McLoughlin and the captain nodded.

Moreover, Iwa-san drew his age when he sailed from Japan. He drew two big circles and eight small circles.

"Oh, Iwa sailed when he was twenty-eight, and he floated more than one year with a broken ship. More than one year ..." Dr. McLoughlin and the captain said, their eyes wet with tears. Dr. McLoughlin stood up and held our shoulders tightly. We couldn't understand his words, but we felt they knew our story like a clear sky.

When I looked out the window, the sun was almost set. The darkness crept over our first day at Fort Vancouver.

~~~~~

We ate a good dinner at Dr. McLoughlin's house. Then they took us to an Englishman's house, which was a one-story three-bedroom house. The Englishman had dark brown eyes, and his Indian wife lived there. The Hudson Bay Company employees were accustomed to marrying Indians. I learned that later.

The couple welcomed us. They took us to a room that had windows in the south and east. There were three beds and two lamps in the room.

"Oh, good beds. They are different from the Cape Indian's third bunk bed," Kyu said.

A mirror hung on the wall, and there was a pitcher with a handle, and three toothbrushes were in three cups. I thought it was not enough water to wash our faces. Sailors gave us a toothbrush when we were in the ship, but we had never seen one before. I didn't feel well with the rough brush in my mouth, so I didn't use it. But we must use it. If we didn't use it, they may not accept us. We must follow their custom, but I still didn't like the toothbrush.

"Good night," the couple said with a soft tone and left.

First, Iwa-san took off his shoes and sat on the bed. We followed Iwa-san.

"I can't stand the shoes. I like zouri or sandal," Kyu complained.

Iwa-san and I agreed, but I said, "We shouldn't say that. They treat us as if we were their guests."

"Yes, indeed," Iwa-san said, nodding. He took off his shirt and pants and changed to pajamas.

"Oh, they are all new," Kyu said like a small boy. "Kenta, without a loincloth, I don't feel comfortable."

I felt strange without a loincloth but knew I must get used to it. I changed to the pajamas.

Iwa-san lay on the bed. We were tired. We had sailed many days, and we reached this village. We didn't understand any of their words. We felt their words were like noisy music or sounded as if we had an ear infection. We tried to change our customs to the Western style. Our nerves were on edge and we couldn't sleep.

"Iwa-san, there are no Mamushi here," I said and put my head on a big pillow.

"There are no Ah-Dank, but as long as humans live, there will be another Mamushi," Iwa-san said.

"Yeah, it's true. They are too kind to us," Kyu said, wondering.

"Hmm ... why are they so kind to us? It is unusual. If we were in Japan, they would put us in jail; then they would investigate. Even though we could go back to our hometown, they would check us thoroughly. But here, they welcomed us to such a beautiful room, smiled, and asked questions as if they were angels. They shed tears for us, too. Moreover they gave us dinner," Iwa-san said with a sigh.

We ate dinner with Dr. McLoughlin, the captain, and other employees of the Hudson Bay Company. The cook gave us a thick soup and then meat, vegetables, and fruit. I felt very uneasy when I saw the bloody meat. In Japan, if we ate an animal that had four legs, we were told that we would go to hell. But we had to eat any leftover food in Cape Flattery in order to survive. We ate salmon and whale meat. Once in a while we ate deer meat, but we had never eaten bloody meat before.

People who eat such bloody meat must be monsters. In the ship, most of the meat was boiled with vegetables. I bit it as if I were eating snakes, but the meat was tasty. Iwa-san ate it all, and Kyu ate half of it. I ate two pieces.

"It's strange," I murmured.

"What?" Kyu asked.

"They ate such meat, but they prayed and said, 'Amen.' If we were in Japan, we couldn't even pray for a while," I said.

"Yes, if we ate an animal that had four legs, our bodies would be dirty for ten days. We couldn't pray to any gods. We must not even think of gods," Kyu said.

"Maybe they prayed for forgiveness because they ate animals. If they pray, their god will forgive them," Kyu guessed.

"But when we arrived, the man prayed. What kind of prayer was that?" I questioned.

"Maybe they thanked their god that we arrived safely," Iwa-san said.

"Hmm ... it was a thank-you prayer. But there are no god altars anywhere; nevertheless, they pray. I can't understand that," I said.

I felt uneasy and looked at the bright lanterns.

~ ~ ~ ~ ~

Sunlight came through the window. We were tired, but we woke up very early.

Mr. Tom Bacon and his wife Jane were still asleep. There was no sound in the house.

"Cock-a-doodle-do!" We heard a rooster's voice.

"Oh, a rooster. It is just like Japan. In Cape Flattery, we had no roosters," Kyu said with a smile.

"Should we go to the purification bath?" Iwa-san suggested.

I realized that I didn't hear any pounding of the waves. I had felt something was different. Now I knew it. I grew up in Onoura, a sea village. Cape Flattery was near the sea. I sailed one year and two months in the ship. I had heard the sound of the sea since I was born. But there were no seas here in Fort Vancouver.

"That is a good idea. There is a big river," Kyu said.

"Shh … do not make a sound. The couple is still sleeping," Iwa-san murmured. We went out with pajamas on and without shoes. It was only one mile to the river. Maple trees made long shadows. It was a fresh morning. We took off our pajamas and jumped into the water. We used to take a bath every day, even though we were sailing in the Pacific. But when we lived in Cape Flattery, we had no time to take a bath because of the many duties we had, such as carrying firewood, drawing water, fishing, making ropes, picking up seaweed, washing, cutting wood, and so on.

Now we felt we were in heaven. We got out from the river and dried our bodies and put on the pajamas.

"We are going to take a bath every day," said Iwa-san.

"We must pray, but there are no god altars," Kyu said.

"Indeed. There are no altars, just the same as Cape Flattery," I said.

"Well, how can I pray, Iwa-san?" Kyu asked.

"Hmm … "

"We must pray to Buddha, Shinto, and Funadama-san, but there is a god here, too. What is their god's name? Amen-san? We must pray to their god as well," I said.

"Okay, we must pray for Amen-san, too," Kyu said.

Most of the sailors were afraid of evil consequences. We knelt by the river and prayed.

"Funadama-san, please protect us and my parents, Hana and Yuki. Amen-san, nice to meet you. Please take care of us," I knelt and prayed silently.

When we went back to the house, there were a few people in the garden. One of them pointed to us and shouted something. Then another man shouted, too.

"We are like a show," Kyu said.

When we were near the Bacons, his wife, Jane, looked at us and shouted in a high tone. Then Mr. Bacon came out and said something with a loud voice.

"What did they say?" I asked.

"Maybe we got up early," said Kyu.

"No, he may be asking where we have been," Iwa-san said.

"We went to bathe and prayed. Nothing to be afraid of," I said.

"Yes, we prayed to Amen-san, too," said Kyu.

Mr. Bacon ran to us and pulled Kyu's hand, and said, "Hurry!"

We all ran into the house.

"You must not go out wearing pajamas. It's shameful," Mr. Bacon said.

We looked at each other, puzzled.

Mr. Bacon pulled Kyu's pajamas and said something in a serious tone.

"Well, our robes must be the problem," Iwa-san said.

I looked my pajamas. There were no holes or dirt. I was not comfortable wearing the pajamas while I was sleeping. We all took them off during the night. We never wore any pajamas when we slept in Japan. We slept with a loincloth or the same kimono we wore in the daytime.

"This is the sleeping clothes. Do not go outside in this. Everyone will laugh at you," Mr. Bacon repeated.

Now we knew we must not go out in pajamas.

~ ~ ~ ~ ~

In the afternoon, Mr. Bacon took us to the fortress. I hadn't recognized it yesterday. "What is that?" Kyu's and my eyes grew wide.

We saw something strange.

"This is a cannon," Iwa-san said.

"Oh, cannon!" I had heard about it, but this is the first time I saw one.

"Who are you going to shoot?" Kyu asked.

"One who did something bad, so we have to be careful," I said.

Iwa-san laughed and said, "Cannons are used for war. There are many other ways to punish bad people, such as hanging, beating, and beheading."

"I see. Then is there any war here?" I asked.

We all looked at the cannon with amazement.

Mr. Bacon looked at us with a smile and stepped up to Dr. McLoughlin's door.

"Come in, come in," he invited us.

Dr. McLoughlin smiled and welcomed us.

"Did you sleep well?" he asked and pretended to sleep.

"Yes, I did," Iwa-san said and motioned a pillow on his head.

While Iwa-san and Dr. McLoughlin were talking, Kyu pointed to an iron box with legs and paws. There were several pieces of wood beside the iron box.

"Look!" Kyu said.

"Oh, there must be wood inside," I responded.

"It must be a stove, but what is that?" Kyu asked and pointed at a chimney.

"Maybe it is used for smoke," I guessed.

"That is a good idea. They are smart," Kyu said.

There was no smoke, so the room didn't get sooty.

Iwa-san was still listening to conversation between Dr. McLoughlin and Mr. Bacon. Of course, Iwa-san couldn't understand their words, but he tried to sense the tone of their conversation.

Later I found out what they were talking about. At first, Dr. McLoughlin thought he was going to send us to Hawaii; then we could board a whaling ship and go home, but he found out Japan was a closed country except for the Dutch and Chinese.

Then he thought we were the first Japanese guests in England. He treated us in a friendly manner, and he wanted us to understand England's power, progress, and present condition. If we knew that England was a great country and talked about it to Japan, Japan and England would be traders in the future. Then our sailing would end up benefiting Japan's future and we would be proud ourselves. So Dr. McLoughlin ordered Mr. Bacon to teach us the English language and Christian love.

When Dr. McLoughlin and Mr. Bacon shook hands, I felt good will from them.

~~~~~

I was scrubbing the floor of Dr. McLoughlin's house, and Kyu was cleaning the window glass. I realized glass windows made the inside of the house so bright. The Cape Indians' houses had no glass windows, so inside their house it was dark. Also my house in Japan was dark inside, but the sun came straight though the window here and we could see outside through the window. It was shocking.

"Kenta, why is there no glass in Japan?" Kyu asked.

"Indeed. If we had glass, our houses would be brighter," I said, nodding.

A month had passed by since we had arrived in Fort Vancouver. We all waited to go back to Japan, but the ship from England came only once a year.

We knew Japan was far away, and with our broken ship, it took fourteen months to come here. If we used a ship with a sail, we might go back to Japan in several months, so we relaxed.

Every morning, we learned English from Mr. Bacon for two hours. Sometimes our study extended to two hours and thirty minutes or three hours. We heard the same words again and again. Soon we could speak greetings and have easy conversations. Mr. Bacon also taught us American customs.

Dr. McLoughlin taught English to French people, Indians, and Russians at his home. They used a special language for business. There were not many European women in Fort Vancouver. Also every Sunday there was Sunday school and worship service at Dr. McLoughlin's house.

While Kyu and I worked on domestic tasks, Iwa-san was working at a shipyard. The Hudson Bay Company was involved in farm work, dairy farms, the lumber business, shipbuilding, and the fur trade.

Kyu and I went to the bread factory. There was a long kneading table in the huge room. The bread factory was very hot like an oven. We got the bread and delivered it. Every time we walked outside, "Kenta, Kyu," the children called, coming to us. Kyu and I sang Japanese children's songs, and the children sang joyfully, too. The children followed us.

I put the bread on the shelves. Ronald and a few children were there.

"Thank you," the master said.

"You are welcome," I said and bowed respectfully.

There were bowls, plates, cloth, boots, leather shoes, silk hats, brooms, cigarettes, lamps, candles, saws, salt, sugar, soap, vinegar, glass bottles, matches, and other items on the shelves.

"Kenta, if you could bring one thing to Japan, what would you like?" Kyu asked.

"Well, I want to have matches. Matches are very convenient. I don't have to use flints anymore. My mother would be very happy. They are like magic," I said. When I saw the fire, I was amazed.

"Kenta, I'd like a glass bottle," Kyu said.

"You really like glass, don't you?" I asked.

"Yes, I love glass." Kyu laughed. "If they said we could have two things, what more would you want?"

"Well, I'd like a blackboard," I answered.

"Who will be pleased with it?" Kyu asked.

"Everyone will be pleased. A teacher and students must like it. After you write with a piece of chalk, you can erase it. There is nothing like that in Japan," I said.

"You are right. Well, I like the soap. It is great for washing our bodies—also kimonos," Kyu said.

"So, how would you translate the word *soap* into Japanese?" I asked.

"*Hayaarai* (first wash)," Kyu said.

"That's not good. How about *akakeshi* (dirt eraser)," I said.

"Kenta, that is a good one." Kyu clapped his hands.

"How about this one?" I asked and pointed out.

"Hmm … I can't remember," Kyu said.

"That is a handsaw," Ronald, who had kissed my cheek before, said with a smile.

"Yes, handsaw. Thank you, Ronald. I have to write it down so when we go back to Japan, I can teach English to my friends," Kyu said.

"Yes," I nodded. Kyu repeated, 'When we go back to Japan.' When we were in Cape Flattery, we didn't say such words.

But can we ever go back to Japan? I felt uneasy.

A Lost Sheep

It was the middle of September, three months since we had arrived in Fort Vancouver. June, July, and August were hot, but now the weather had turned cold.

"September." I opened my notebook. I had written so many words, and I opened it every time I had a chance. I loved to learn. Every day I learned something new.

Iwa-san was shaving with a bar of soap. Captain Jumon had shaved without soap. He didn't even know about soap, lather, and the glass mirror.

If everyone had survived …

"Cold today," Kyu complained.

"Iwa-san, I don't like the bathroom here. I have to sit on the toilet bowl. I don't feel well. I am still not accustomed to it," I said.

"Indeed, I don't like it, either. When I came here, I had constipation for a while," Iwa-san said.

"The Cape Indians' bathroom was just like in Japan. Dig the hole and put a branch on the top. It was simple," I said.

"Yes, we could also enjoy birds singing. It was peaceful," Kyu said with a smile.

"I don't hear the birds singing when I use the bathroom here," I said.

~ ~ ~ ~ ~

We had had so many surprises since we came to Fort Vancouver.

Every seventh day, all the village people went to Dr. McLoughlin's house and worshiped. The shipyard, offices, farms, and stores were all closed. We felt it was a very strange custom.

"Are their businesses all right?" Kyu wondered.

In Japan, businesses closed the first and fifteenth of every month and on the New Year. We were all puzzled why they had to rest every seventh day.

"But if we worked from morning to night every day, we would be tired. So it's a good custom, but if we have no Sunday school, we will have off all day. That is strange," Kyu said, tilting his head.

We went to the church. At first we didn't understand anything, but as our English improved a little, we could understand better.

Later I learned that in England, in the middle of seventeenth century, there was a regulation that ordered all the businesses to close on Sunday, Christmas, and Easter. But this regulation was only for one century. The Industrial Revolution broke the regulation. People had to work fourteen to seventeen hours a day in 1833, after the Factory Law was passed in England. We arrived in Fort Vancouver the year after the Factory Law passed.

Dr. McLoughlin was a true Christian, so he opened his house for services every Sunday. His house was like an official residence rather than a private residence.

In Sunday school, we always sat in the back seats. The organ started and then everyone sang the hymns. Children sang loudly. Then Dr. McLoughlin prayed; the Bible was read. We understood "God is love." God is like Buddha or Amateras Omikami (Shintoism.)

A teacher put a colorful box on the table, and then he opened the curtains on the box. A stir ran through the children.

A lost sheep was under a cliff. The teacher moved the sheep and cried, "Ba, ba." The sheep tried to climb the cliff, but he slipped down many times.

"This sheep was lost from his flock. There were one hundred sheep, but this poor sheep was the only one that was lost." The teacher talked slowly and clearly, so the children could understand. The sheep cried as if he were a lost child.

"Where are you?" a man asked.

The sheep heard the voice. "Ba, ba," he cried.

Then the man came down from the cliff.

"This man is Jesus Christ," the teacher said.

"This is a puppet show," Kyu said.

"Yes." I nodded and watched Jesus, who tried to hold the branches and stones. Then he came down slowly.

Everyone wished for him to come down safely.

Jesus called to the sheep, "I am coming, so you will be safe." Jesus' movement was excellent. All the children watched his every step. At last, Jesus reached the bottom of the cliff. The children clapped their hands.

The sheep cried. The doll's hand patted the sheep's head. The children felt as if Jesus' hand patted their head.

Jesus held the sheep on his shoulders. "You are safe now. Let's go back to your flock," the teacher said with a gentle voice. Then the Jesus doll started going up the cliff. Finally, Jesus reached the top of the cliff.

I thought it was over, but the scene changed.

"This is Golgotha," the teacher said with a deep voice.

Jesus was laid on the cross, and his one hand was nailed to the cross.

"Oh, painful!" Kyu shouted.

Then the children looked back at him.

Another hand was nailed and then his feet, too.

"Cruel!" Kyu shouted again.

The children turned around again.

After Jesus was nailed to the cross, the cross was raised; the sheep and other dolls came down to the cross.

"Jesus! You saved me. You are a kind man. Why do you have to die on the cross?" The sheep looked at Jesus and cried.

The children nodded.

The teacher said, "Everyone, why did Jesus die on the cross? Did he have sins? No, he died for our sins."

"Crucifixion is meant for a wicked man," Kyu remarked.

"Kenta, Kyu, this may be what it means to be Christian," Iwa-san whispered.

Oh! Christian! I felt goose bumps. In Japan, if someone became a Christian, the entire family was beheaded.

"Is it true, Iwa-san?" Kyu asked.

"I think so," Iwa-san said and crossed his arms.

We didn't know whether Dr. McLoughlin was Christian. We didn't have any knowledge about Christianity.

Christianity was forbidden 250 years ago in Japan. Iwa-san had heard this when he sailed on a ship a long time ago. One of the sailors told him some secret Christian group lived in his village. Their symbol was a cross. The chief Christian was nailed on the cross. When Iwa-san watched the puppet show, he remembered the story that he had heard before.

"We thought their god was Amen-san, but it was Christian. What should we do?" I asked.

"Well, we must not believe it even though we just heard the story," Kyu said.

"Too many problems, Iwa-san," I said and sighed.

"Jesus is the true savior. You must accept Him," the teacher said, but we didn't care any longer.

~ ~ ~ ~ ~

When Lord Hashiba governed all of Japan, everyone obeyed him, except one Christian girl. She was a girl from Arima, who didn't follow his orders. She preferred to die gladly rather than to obey him.

"This Christian girl wasn't afraid of death for her God," Hashiba said; he was scared of her God, Jesus Christ. Then Hashiba oppressed the Christians.

In 1639, many Christians were killed, but still some Christians lived secretly.

Most Japanese people were afraid of being Christian.

~ ~ ~ ~ ~

"Iwa-san, we must not attend Sunday school anymore. I will have a stomachache next Sunday," Kyu said and touched his stomach.

"But how about the following Sunday?" Iwa-san asked.

"Well, I will catch a cold," responded Kyu.

"Kyu, if you get sick every Sunday, they will find out it was faked," Iwa-san said.

"But even if we didn't attend Sunday school, Dr. McLoughlin wouldn't nail me to a cross," Kyu said.

A cow mooed in the field.

"Oh, a cow doesn't have to go worship. I wish I were a cow," Kyu said.

"It's a problem," Iwa-san said; his eyes darkened. "When we go back to Japan, we will be asked about Christianity. Even though we haven't changed our religion, they will ask."

"Yes, that is scary," Kyu said; his face turned blue like sea water.

"But Christians are not as bad as the Japanese officials," Iwa-san commented.

"Iwa-san, if the Japanese officials heard such things, you would be killed," I warned.

"I know," Iwa-san said and made a bitter smile. "Kenta, Kyu, think carefully. If Christianity is a bad religion, they would not treat us so well."

"Indeed, Mr. Bacon and Dr. McLoughlin are very kind. In Japan, no officials treat us as well as they do," I said.

"Yes, we heard that Christians drank blood, or ate human flesh, but I can't believe such things," Kyu said.

"Yes, but even if it is a good religion, we must not believe it," I demanded.

"Yes, the important thing is we must follow the rules, good or bad; it doesn't matter," Kyu agreed.

"Of course, but if it is a good religion, we should listen while we are here," Iwa-san suggested.

"Iwa-san! Don't say that. We are afraid of the punishment when we go back to Japan," Kyu and I implored.

Iwa-san nodded, but his mind was elsewhere.

~~~~~

It was Sunday morning.

"Ouch!"

"Ouch!"

Kyu and I moaned in the bed. We didn't go to eat breakfast, so Mr. and Mrs. Bacon came to our room. As soon as Kyu saw them, he moaned, "Ouch! Ouch!"

"What is the matter with you?" they asked and ran to Kyu and me. We held our stomachs.

"Oh, you have stomachaches. That is too bad," Mr. Bacon said, putting his hand on my stomach. When I saw Mr. Bacon's blue eyes, I felt sorry. But I was frantic.

Iwa-san said, "As long as we live here, we must attend the church worship service."

But I didn't want to hear anything about Jesus' story. When I went back to Japan, if the Japanese officials thought I had become a Christian, my parents and my sweet sister Hana would die on the cross or be burned alive. I wanted to keep away from Jesus as much as possible. Even Buddha said, "Circumstances sometimes justify a lie." Still I felt guilty when Mr. Bacon looked worried about me. But now I felt my stomach really begin to hurt.

"I will call a doctor," Mr. Bacon said, and they left the room.

"What did Mr. Bacon say?" Kyu asked.

"Call a doctor," I answered and sat on the bed.

"Oh! Is a doctor coming? What shall I do, Iwa-san?" Kyu shouted.

"Just keep on pretending to have a stomachache," said Iwa-san.

"I think so, too," Kyu and I agreed and lay on the bed, meek as lambs.

Soon Mr. Bacon came with a short French man with sparkling eyes like a cat.

"He is the best doctor in Fort Vancouver," Mr. Bacon introduced him. At that time, French medical methods were the most advanced in the world.

I see. He is the doctor. There were no doctors in my hometown, Onoura, Japan. Even my father had only taken herb medication for his leg and hip pain. While the doctor examined us, I felt tense. The doctor asked several questions.

"What did you give them for supper last night?" the doctor asked.

"Soup, beef, bread, and onions," Mrs. Bacon answered.

"Did you eat the same meal?" the doctor asked.

"Yes," said Mrs. Bacon.

"I see. It is not because of the supper," the doctor said.

I was afraid the doctor would find out our stomachaches were faked. Then the doctor used a pipe made with a thick paper to listen to our chests.

What is it? I wondered. The doctor put the pipe onto Kyu's chest, and he put his ear to other end of the pipe, and listened. *Can he tell everything?* My heart beat like a drum. Kyu twisted his face and moaned.

"Do you have pain? That is too bad," the doctor said and removed the pipe from Kyu's stomach. "Did you eat something else?"

Kyu and I pretended that we didn't understand what he said.

"We can't communicate," the doctor said to Mr. Bacon. Then he put the pipe on my body. "Oh, his heartbeat is too fast. Well, I think they are not too bad. Give them only soup. Later we will see," the doctor said and left the room.

"Well, how about church?" Kyu asked.

"Oh, no!" Mr. Bacon shook his hand. "You need rest today. Sleep well. Iwa-san, come to eat breakfast with us. Kyu and Kenta must not eat until night," Mr. Bacon said and left.

"It's well done!" Kyu smiled after the door closed.

"Iwa-san, you must go to breakfast," I suggested.

"Only I can eat breakfast," Iwa-san said, smiling, and left the room.

"What? Can't we eat breakfast?" Kyu asked.

"Not until supper," I answered.

"Until supper? Oh, no. If I don't eat breakfast, I will faint. Oh, no!" Kyu said, almost crying.

"We won't die if we skip our two meals. As long as I don't have to attend the worship service, I will be glad," I said.

"Yes, that's true. But we must not use a stomachache next time," Kyu suggested.

"But even if we had a headache, it would still be the same. We can't eat like normal people when we are sick," I said.

"Indeed. But why do the Japanese officials oppress Christianity? Kenta, we must pray to any god. Don't you think so?" Kyu asked.

"Yes, but it is forbidden. We have to obey the Japanese officials. I don't want to lose my head," I said.

"We are nonbelievers. Why do they have to behead us?" Kyu asked.

"No, if the Japanese officials think we are Christians, they will give us an extremely hard punishment," I said.

"Most Japanese know Christianity is a scary religion. Even if we live in a Western country, they should understand that we wouldn't believe Christianity," Kyu said.

"They can't understand. But, Kyu, was the man who saved the sheep Jesus? The god?" I asked.

"Why did the god die on the cross?" Kyu asked.

"The man who saved the sheep seemed to be a good man. I don't know if Jesus Christ is a god or human, but he must be a very good man," I said.

"Yes, but it was only doll's play," Kyu said.

"But we have been hearing the name Jesus Christ. I didn't know Jesus Christ was related to Christianity. I just thought Amen-san was a person. What does Amen mean?" I asked.

"I don't know. Oh, I am so hungry. Kenta, this must be punishment from heaven because we pretended to be sick," Kyu said and sighed like a lost sheep.

"It's hard to lie in bed without a stomachache," Kyu murmured.

I looked at the sky though the window. *The sky is the same in Onoura and here.*

"Iwa-san," Kyu said.

"What?" Iwa-san answered, sitting on the bed.

"I can't get sick next Sunday. I am too hungry to have a fake sickness," Kyu said.

"Even if you don't eat one or two meals, do not complain. When we were in the storms, we couldn't sleep or eat," Iwa-san said.

"That is true. When we were in the storms, I didn't even think I was hungry. It was mysterious," Kyu said.

"Oh, I couldn't believe it myself. I didn't know where my strength came from to cut down the mast," Iwa-san said, breathing deeply.

I listened to Kyu and Iwa-san's conversation. Iwa-san cut the mast while it was storming. "Watch out!" Captain Jumon had shouted. Masa and Kazuo's faces appeared briefly. *Everyone died.* It was a miracle that we still lived.

Raindrops hit the window.

"Oh, it is raining. The church service must be over," Kyu said and looked at the wall clock.

"It is only ten past ten. Church service will be finished at eleven," I said.

We had never seen a clock until we came to Fort Vancouver. We asked what it was, but we couldn't figure it out. They said it told the time, but we couldn't see the time, so it was hard to understand. But gradually, we learned that the hands of the clock showed something. When we went to the church, Mr. Bacon pointed at the clock and said, "It nine o'clock. Time to go to the church."

Then we finally found out the clock was a time-telling machine.

"Oh, I am hungry. I want to eat something. I will go to the kitchen and eat," Kyu said.

"Kyu, all the food is the Bacons'. It's not yours," Iwa-san said with a strict voice.

"But they prepared it for us. So I will tell them later," Kyu said and pouted.

"No, if you take someone's things, it's like being a robber," Iwa-san said.

"It's not being a robber. I will tell them later. Kenta, what do you think?" Kyu asked.

"Kyu, I agree with Iwa-san. Even if you are hungry, you must not steal their food," I said.

"Okay. Oh, I am hungry," Kyu said and almost cried on the bed.

Iwa-san and I looked at each other and laughed.

"Iwa-san, I don't want to fake being sick anymore. I will attend the church service next Sunday," Kyu said.

"Church …" I murmured; I was still afraid of going to the church. "Well, we are in the Christian land. Even if we attend the church or not, the Japanese officials will ask strict questions," I said with a sigh.

"Yes, Kenta, when we go back to Japan, we can say we didn't become Christian. We don't have to say that we attended the church service," Iwa-san said.

I was still afraid of the Japanese officials, but what could I do?

"Worrying is not good for our health. Think positive. We must pray to our gods for our safety," Iwa-san concluded.

Captain Jumon and Commander Roku prayed hard, but the gods didn't hear their wishes. Which god should I pray to? This was a Christian country. I felt I couldn't depend on my Japanese gods while I was in the Christian land. I turned my eyes to the window.

"Oh! Who are those children?" I shouted.

Mr. and Mrs. Bacon walked toward to the house with umbrellas, and the children followed them.

In Japan, an umbrella was made with thick oiled paper. We all liked Japanese umbrellas. Every time the rain hit the oil paper umbrella, it made pleasant sounds. We loved these sounds.

Many umbrellas kept on coming.

"Oh, Da-Ka and Ronald, too," Kyu said.

I sat up on the bed and saw the children through the window. Soon someone knocked on the door, and Mrs. Bacon came into the room and said. "How do you feel? Many children came to visit you."

The children followed Da-Ka and walked in. They smiled shyly and gave us wild flowers or pictures. Then they sang in ringing voices. Their cheeks were red as apples.

They must be Christian songs. Is this a custom in this country? I felt it was beautiful. I had never heard of bringing flowers and pictures, or visiting or singing for sick people. *If Japanese village children would visit my father and sing for him, he might be very pleased,* I thought.

Soon the children finished singing. "Let us pray," Da-Ka said.

"What shall I do?" Kyu asked and looked at Iwa-san and me.

"Calm down!" Iwa-san whispered.

"But Christians pray ..." Kyu murmured.

Da-Ka prayed for healing our stomachs, God's blessing, and comforting us. I understood Da-Ka's words.

They are normal words. Not magic, but kind words. I felt relieved; then I felt guilty looking upon the children's pure eyes.

Christianity is not too bad.

After Da-Ka prayed, each child prayed, one after another. They said, "Amen," at the end.

"What does Amen mean?" I asked.

"It is true," Da-Ka answered.

"I thought Amen was a god's name," I said.

Da-Ka and all the children laughed.

"Do you still have pain?" Ronald asked.

"No more pain," I answered.

"Good. Let play puzzles," Ronald said.

Ronald always brought games. He taught us to use toy building blocks, hula-hoops, and puzzles. Kyu was very good at the hula-hoop. We were hungry, but we enjoyed playing the games.

"It's noon. Time to go home," Da-Ka suggested.

The children wanted to play longer, but Da-Ka said, "No!"

Ronald hugged my neck and said, "Kenta, don't be sick anymore and come to church." He kissed my cheek again.

I held back my tears.

EAGLE

I still remember the first time I saw the *Eagle*, 295 feet in length and 21,350 square feet. I thought the English warship, the *Eagle*, was four times larger than the *Takaramaru*.

"Just like a little castle!" we said in amazement.

The night before, Dr. McLoughlin introduced Captain Wise, the captain of the *Eagle*, to us. We were going back to Japan. The children sang farewell songs for us. Their voices touched my heart. But Ronald's voice changed to a sob. Then all the children cried. Mixed blood children especially loved us, perhaps because of our yellow skins. We were their heroes. When the children cried, Kyu and I shed our tears. Even Iwa-san bit his lips, looking at the chandelier.

Now we were at the Bacons'. Mr. Bacon gave each of us a black square trunk.

"The trunk is very strong," I said.

"But I like the wicker suitcase better," Kyu said.

"But there are pockets, a key, and a handle. Also I can sit on it," I said.

"But wind does not penetrate it," said Kyu.

We put our things into the trunk. A comb, notebook, pencils, pajamas, shirts, pants, a toothbrush, a jacket. *When we left Cape Flattery, we didn't have anything.*

Iwa-san was silent; his face was pale. I felt uneasy. *If the* Eagle, *the warship, goes to Japan, what will the Japanese officials think about?* I had goose bumps.

Dr. McLoughlin prayed before the dinner. Mr. and Mrs. Bacon

and officers of the *Eagle* sat at the table with us. The last dinner at Fort Vancouver began.

The first time we saw the shiny silverware, we didn't know what to do. In Japan, we could eat everything with only chopsticks. Why did they have to use so many forks, spoons, and a knife? But we learned their manner in six months. I also learned to eat soup without making any sound.

After the dinner, a big globe was placed on the table.

"Iwa, Kenta, Kyu. This is Fort Vancouver. This is the Columbia River, and this is the Pacific Ocean." Dr. McLoughlin turned the globe, and his finger pointed and he said, "This is Japan."

Finally, we are going back to Japan.

"The *Eagle* goes here first," Dr. McLoughlin said and pointed out Hawaii.

We nodded. We thought the *Eagle* would go from Hawaii to Japan, but then he pointed to Cape Horn, South America.

Where are we going?

Dr. McLoughlin turned his head to us and said, "This is England. The *Eagle* goes to London; then it goes to South Africa, to Macao, then to Japan. It will take one year to reach Japan."

Why don't they go straight to Japan? I felt dizzy.

~ ~ ~ ~ ~

It was misty morning. Many people came to the port to say farewell, but their faces were hazy. We couldn't see Tacoma Fuji, either, but when we went back to Japan, we would see the real Mt. Fuji.

When I was in Onoura, Japan, I had never thought about Fort Vancouver. I didn't even know it existed. I had never thought there were such wonderful people in a foreign country. Dr. McLoughlin and the Cape Indians cared for us. They gave us food, clothes, and beds. *People are thoughtful.*

"This ship is huge," Kyu said, amazed.

"Yes," I said, looking at the three masts. The sailors climbed to the sailing yard. Their hips were big like watermelons. Each sailor had good muscles, and they seemed much stronger than us.

Iwa-san had become cheerful like a fish in the water since he was on the ship. "I really am a sailor. My heart is jumping around," he said and left. *He must be going to check all over the inside of the* Eagle.

England's warships were classified depending on the number of cannons. The first class warship must carry at least one hundred cannons. Ninety to one hundred cannons was a second class warship. The *Eagle* had fifty cannons, and it ranked fourth class.

"This English warship is great. The bottom of the ship is covered by copper, Kenta!" Kyu's voice was excited.

"Mr. Bacon said in order to protect the bottom of the ship, they use copper. Before that they used iron nails. Then it started to rust," I said.

"I see; then now what kind of nails are they using?" Kyu asked.

"Iron nails are still used, but they are covered by copper. The *Takaramaru* used a copper board," I said; I remembered that the white board of the *Takaramaru* with the blue-green copper board was beautiful. I narrowed my eyes.

Even though the ships bottom was covered by copper, a little sea water still accumulated in the bottom of the ship; therefore, the sailors removed the sea water using four chain pumps.

Iwa-san worked as a carpenter, Kyu did other chores, and I was a chef's helper. We were quite busy, so we met only at meal time and before we slept. The sailors slept in the hammocks. There were not only beds hanging, but also tables and chairs hung down when they ate.

At last we were on a ship again. We didn't have to go to church anymore. The fog cleared and we saw the blue sea.

"Oh, look! Sea!" Kyu shouted as if he were a kid.

"Yes, I missed it!" I felt moved to tears. The sea scared me, but this sea connected to Japan. Tears rolled down my cheeks.

Twenty days had passed by since we sailed. The ship was headed to Hawaii. It was getting hot.

"Baa, baa …" the sheep were crying. There were two cages at the bow; I saw two sheep, three chickens, and five pigs there.

"Are you hungry?" I asked them.

"Baa, baa …" the sheep cried again. I saw the sheep's gentle eyes.

You will be eaten. I felt sad. These animals belonged to the officers. Once in a while, the chicken had eggs. Only the officers ate such things. Our food was always very simple. The *Eagle* carried lime juice for preventing scurvy. "Limey" meant an English sailor at that time.

The first time we saw canned food was at Mr. Bacon's house.

"This was invented by the French," Mr. Bacon said, and he explained how to make canned food.

If we had had canned food when we were on the Takaramaru, *it would have been convenient.* We all felt that way. We were all amazed by the advanced technique.

"Baa, baa ..." when I saw the gentle eyes of the sheep, I remembered the doll play at Dr. McLoughlin's house. Jesus Christ saved the sheep from the steep hill and he died on the cross. I thought we would have no more church meetings. But I was very surprised. The first Sunday morning on the *Eagle*, we were called, along with two hundred sailors, onto the deck. *What will happen?* I wondered. The captain spoke and then read the Bible. The captain prayed, and then we sang hymns.

"Wow, the chapel in the ship. We can't escape," Kyu said and dropped his shoulders.

"Christianity is a very strong religion," I said and sighed, too. "Are there any Funadama-san in the *Eagle*?"

"I don't think so. Everyone seems Christian," Kyu said.

That night, Kyu and I cried in bed, and Iwa-san seemed worried.

If the Christian warship carries us to Japan, will the Japanese officials accept us?

~ ~ ~ ~ ~

Sailors drank rum and relaxed on Sunday afternoon. Only at Sunday lunch was alcohol given to the sailors. Several sailors danced on the deck. Some sang wearing red and white shirts. Some were half naked. One sailor played the violin.

"Very soon, the plum trees will be in bloom," a sailors said.

"Soon, the New Year is coming," I said.

"I want to eat mochi," Kyu said with his mouth watering.

"Mochi is good, but I want to eat fish. Even though we saw a lot of fish swimming in the sea, no one wants to catch them," Iwa-san said.

It was hard to cook fish for two hundred people, and it smelled fishy. It was impossible to cook with only one chef and several helpers. When we were on the *Takaramaru*, we could eat miso soup, fish, and vegetables. We were only fourteen sailors, so Master Chef Goro could manage it. Now we were given one pound of dried bread a day.

Monday: One pound of salted pork, butter, bread.

Tuesday: Two pounds of salted beef, bread.

Wednesday: Beans, oatmeal, sugar, butter, bread.

Thursday: One pound of salted pork, bread.

Friday: Beans, oatmeal, sugar, butter, bread.

Saturday: Two pounds of salted beef, bread.

Sunday: Beans, oatmeal, sugar, alcohol, bread.

We all wanted to eat fish rather than the meat and rice rather than dried bread.

The sailors had to bring their own silverware and plates. Most of the sailors had no silverware. They ate with their hands. Only officers had forks, knives, and spoons. The sailors used jackknives when they had to cut the meat. We had no soup. The cook sold the leftover meat soaked in water as soup. The sailors dipped the hard bread into the warm water and ate. The sailors had no uniforms; they had to buy their own clothes.

"Everyone is spineless!" Ben, who had skeleton tattoos on his arm, shouted. Kyu and I called him Skeleton. He had sharp eyes and his lips were curved down. He was a popular guy, and many sailors were fond of him. He always talked loudly.

"Don't you think so?" He looked around at the sailors. Every time Ben talked, the sailors clapped their hands.

"We are not different from the captain. We have two eyes, two ears, and one mouth. We are both humans!" Ben said.

Between the main masts, the officers stayed at the stern and the sailors were gathered at the bow. Even though a sailor shouted loud, the officers in the stern couldn't hear it.

"You know, our stomachs are not different from the officers. Not only the officers' stomachs need beef steaks," Ben said.

The sailors sipped the rum and nodded joyfully.

"I can't speak loudly," Ben lowered his voice.

The sailors stooped and listened.

"Two hundred sailors are controlled by only ten officers? It is a strange thing," Ben noticed.

The sailors looked at each other and nodded. They could relax only on Sunday afternoon. For six days, they were shouted at, ordered around, and beaten by the officers.

"Indeed. So many sailors were hanged under the yard. We don't have too much whipping nowadays," one sailor said.

"Yeah, a ship is the same as a jail. Even though we want to escape, it is all water. It is the perfect jail without a fence," Ben said.

Iwa-san, Kyu, and I listened. We could almost understand what they said.

"Do you remember, an executive trainer came from London? We had a storm," Ben said.

"Oh, he was seasick. The captain tied him to the mast for many days as a punishment. It was pitiful," the sailor with a flat nose said.

"An executive trainer must be punished once in a while. It's good," a skinny sailor said.

"I heard a two-year-old boy registered in the navy," Ben said.

"Only two years old?" a man who had a long nose asked, rolling his eyes.

"Oh, if he was registered for a long time, he would get better promotions. Of course, he hid his age," Ben said.

"Then what happened to the kid?" the long-nosed man asked.

"His father was rich. He spent money on important connections. The kid became the post captain when he was seventeen," Ben said.

"Only seventeen! It is not fair!" everyone yelled.

"Don't you think it's ridiculous?" Ben asked.

"We have no choice. We were not born into a rich family. It's our sin," said a man who was weak-looking and had bleary eyes.

"Are you stupid?" Ben shouted and spat his saliva.

The weak-looking man's shoulders trembled, and he said, "But I have no choice. My dad, my granddad and my great-granddad were all poor."

"Why is that your sin?" Ben grunted at the man.

"I don't know, but I feel that way," the man said and shook his head.

"That is why I get angry. You and the kid who was registered at two are both humans. If all two hundred sailors got together and fought …" Ben said.

At the moment, a man of about fifty said, "Ben, you better change the subject. How about women?"

We didn't know his name. Everyone called him Dad. He had brown hair, a bald forehead, and gentle blue eyes. He always smiled like Mona Lisa.

Dad said calmly, "Ben, better talk about women."

"Women?" Ben asked.

"Yes," said Dad.

"Okay, Dad. I don't like to talk about women. Someone else take over," Ben said. He wasn't against Dad. Dad was referred to as our captain, or another captain.

Dad was a normal man to me. He was not too strong or extremely handsome. I didn't understand why the sailors called him *our captain.*

The captain was the absolute ruler. Once Captain Wise showed up on the deck, all the officers stood straight. Captain Wise didn't make any jokes to the officers, and even if he invited them for dinner, he didn't get closer to any officers in order to keep his dignity. It was an intelligent method. Also, the officers didn't get close to the sailors. A border at the main mast separated the officers and sailors into different worlds. The sailors didn't say, "Yes, sir." When the sailors responded to a superior, they said, "Aye, aye, sir," which they obeyed the superiors completely. The officers often hit the sailors with a club. So the sailors were always afraid of the officers. The sailors answered, "Aye, aye, sir," and walked in very carefully.

The sailors didn't have to say, "Aye, aye, sir," to Dad, but all the rough fellows obeyed Dad.

"Women? All women are almost the same," a man with bloodshot eyes from drink said.

They started talking about women. Only Ben seemed bored and looked at the sky. Then he turned his eyes to us. "Kids! Do you have fun talking about women?" Ben asked and looked at us with a cold, piercing gaze.

Kyu and I looked at each other; we couldn't answer.

"Of course, women stories are fun," Iwa-san said in Japanese.

"What?" Ben raised his eyebrows.

"I don't love many women, but women stories are interesting," Iwa-san spoke in English this time.

Ben stood up and came closer and asked, "Do you like rum?"

"So-so," Iwa-san answered, and he raised his cup high.

"What is your name?" Ben asked.

"Iwa," Iwa-san said.

"How about you?" Ben asked, looking at Kyu and me.

"Kenta," I said.

"Kyu," Kyu said.

"You are lucky men. Your broken ship reached America. But be careful. You must say 'Aye, aye, sir.' If you make any mistakes, the officers will hit you with a club," Ben said, laughing with a wry mouth.

~ ~ ~ ~ ~

The waves were high. The *Eagle* vibrated all day. The wind blew through the sails. The sun almost dipped to the horizon. The sea changed to a lemon color from blue.

Iwa-san, Kyu, and I were taken by the officer to see Captain Wise.

Why does the captain call us? I didn't think we did anything wrong.

In a few days, the *Eagle* would reach Hawaii. I looked at Kyu. He seemed worried. Only Iwa-san walked calmly. We wore our coats and shoes. It was hot, but to see the captain, we had to dress in our finest clothes.

We stood at the captain's door. The officer knocked and said, "I brought them."

"Okay, you can leave," the captain said. His voice was dignified.

Captain Wise let us enter his room. He smiled. Captain Wise rarely smiled, so when I saw his smiling face, I felt relieved.

"Sit down," Captain Wise said and pointed to the long chairs.

Kyu sat down. Iwa-san bowed and sat. I followed Iwa-san and sat down.

There was a cannon in his room. The sunset came through the window. His overcoat hung on the wall, but during a fight, the wall could be removed. Captain Wise sat; his back was to the wall. Between the captain and us, there was a table. The table's legs were fixed on the floor. There were several hollows on the table to set cups.

"Are you getting used to being here?" Captain Wise spoke slowly.

"Yes, I am," I answered, because Iwa-san was silent.

"One month has passed. Do you have any hardships?" Captain Wise asked.

"Not at all," Iwa-san answered with his gloomy voice.

This ship is scary, I wanted to shout. I couldn't stand to see the officers hit the sailors' shoulders or hips with clubs. It was much more painful than Ah-Dank's whip in Cape Flattery. We were not just sailors; we were guests of the Hudson Bay Company. Therefore, they treated us differently. But we had to follow their strict rules. We had tension every day.

"I see; you are getting used to being here," Captain Wise said and lit his pipe.

"You were also sailors, but not soldiers, right?" Captain Wise asked.

"Yes, we were just sailors," said Iwa-san.

"Oh, can you write your names?" Captain Wise asked.

"Yes, we can," Iwa-san said.

"Really!" Captain Wise put a paper and a pencil on the desk. Iwa-san wrote his name in kanji, Chinese characters. The captain looked at it curiously. "Can you write, too?" Captain Wise asked Kyu.

"Yes, it is easy," he answered. Kyu wrote his name.

"How about you?" Captain Wise asked me.

"Yes, I can," I answered quietly and wrote my name.

Captain Wise held the paper and looked at it a while. He smiled softly and said, "Japan is a wonderful country. All of you can write your names. Many English sailors can't write their names."

We had noticed. Soon after we were on the *Eagle*, we had to write our names, but half of the sailors couldn't write theirs. They just wrote cross signs, which meant they were Christian.

"Would you tell me about Japan?" Captain Wise asked.

"Of course. What kind of things do you want to know?" asked Iwa-san.

"Well, who governs in Japan?" Captain Wise asked.

"It is the shogun," Iwa-san said in Japanese; then he said, "Kenta, what is shogun in English?"

"Well, *head* or *boss*," I said.

"*Head* is not the correct word," Iwa-san said.

"How about Tokugawa shogun?" Kyu said.

"But we have the emperor, too," I said.

"Maybe the captain asked who the most powerful man in Japan is," Iwa-san said.

"Would you please give me a pencil and paper?" Iwa-san asked Captain Wise with very polite English, which Mr. Bacon taught him.

The captain looked at Iwa-san, surprised, and placed a new paper and pencil before him. Iwa-san drew a man's picture and said, "He is an emperor, like a king." Then he drew another man's picture on the other side. "He is Tokugawa shogun. Japan's emperor was a figurehead, a symbolic only. He had no military power, but was under the protection of a shogun, the military leader who actually govern Japan."

"Hmm ... a shogun and a king," Captain Wise said and tilted his head. "Do you have military?"

"Yes," Iwa-san answered and drew a samurai riding with a horse.

"Oh, the cavalry. Do they have any guns?" Captain Wise asked.

"Yes," I said.

"Is there any navy?" Captain Wise asked.

We looked at each other. Our navy was far different from the English navy. But were samurai riding on a warship called the navy? We didn't have huge warships like the *Eagle*. No large ships sailed out of Japan, but there were small ships in Japan. So we said, "Yes."

"Oh, you have a navy as well," Captain Wise said and nodded.

But I thought his idea of Japan was far from the reality. Our limited English was still not enough to explain about Japan.

"Are there any schools?" Captain Wise asked.

"Yes, we have schools," I said.

"Many schools?" Captain Wise asked.

"Yes," I said.

"How about an industry?" Captain Wise asked.

We didn't understand the question.

"Are there any machines?" Captain Wise asked.

"Oh, yes. We have looms," Kyu answered.

The sun set, and the room was getting dark. We heard a pipe that gave the sailors many orders on the deck.

A duty sailor came and lit the whale oil lamp.

"Hmm ... eating rice every day. Eccentric hairstyles. Taking off the shoes when they go in the house," Captain Wise said, looking at the picture of *geta* and *zori*, Japanese slippers. "An interesting country." He seemed fascinated. "You want to go home, don't you?" Captain Wise asked.

We all bowed our heads. I felt almost like crying, thinking about my home country and family.

Captain Wise changed the subject.

"By the way, you talked with Ben on Sunday afternoon?" the captain asked in a casual manner. I was surprised that some watcher always observed us.

"Yes," Iwa-san said.

"What did Ben talk about?" Captain Wise asked.

"Well …" Iwa-san looked in the captain's eyes and said, "It was not a very important thing."

"He asked our names and …" Kyu started saying something, but Iwa-san said, "Oh, yes, our names, rum, and women."

"Is that all?" asked Captain Wise.

"Yes," said Iwa-san.

"Did you see the scar on Ben's back?" Captain Wise asked.

"Yes," Kyu said, nodding.

"Did you hear that story?" Captain Wise asked.

"No, I didn't," Iwa-san said clearly.

I looked at Iwa-san. Ben said it was the scar from the ship punishment. Because he didn't say, "Aye, aye, sir." He was rebellious. Ben also said the ship was a fenceless jail. Now I knew what Captain Wise wanted to know. *Iwa-san is great.*

"Well, two years ago, a baby …" Kyu started talking.

He was going to tell the story of the two-year-old boy registered to the navy who became a captain in his teens. I tapped Kyu's back.

"Yes, the baby died," Iwa-san said instantly.

Now Kyu understood why I tapped his back.

"Yeah, yeah," Kyu said in Japanese.

"I see. Is that all? Anyway, many sailors are rough fellows," Captain Wise said. Then he ordered the duty sailor to bring him a cup of coffee that was made from toasted wheat flour.

The sailors had severe working conditions, were treated cruelty, and were paid a low salary. Once in a while there were volunteers, but not too many men wanted to be sailors. So the Shanghai gang appeared at the English ports and beat them with a club or terrified them with a knife. They kidnapped men from the bars: vagabonds, beggars, or merchant sailors. Some men were beaten unconscious. When they woke up, they were on the ship. "Aye, aye, sir" was an unwritten law, but it was difficult to get the sailors to obey in their hearts. There were a lot of rebellions in the sixteenth and seventeenth centuries. In 1830, there was not too much violence against sailors, but still the sailors were an outrageous group.

Captain Wise always saw Ben as a dangerous man.

CHRISTMAS

It was a calm sea. The sun hit the *Eagle*, hot like fire.

The rooster crowed on the deck.

"The rooster is for the officers' Christmas dinner," Ben said with a snicker.

All the sailors were polishing the cannons with rags. Ben always picked the bow, where far away from the officers. Polishing the cannon was not hard work. While we were working, we still could talk in a low voice.

"What is Christmas?" I asked.

"Oh, don't you know about Christmas?" Ben raised his eyebrows.

"No, I don't," I said.

"This is shocking. There was no Christmas in Japan?" Ben shrugged his shoulders and said, "Dad, there is no Christmas in Japan."

"Really? But the world is so big," Dad said with a smile.

"Please tell me what Christmas is," I asked.

Ben looked at me and said, "God's Son, Jesus Christ's birthday."

"Oh! The Christian's festival!" Kyu shouted.

"Well then, is Jesus Christ the Son of God?" I asked.

"I have never seen him. I do not even celebrate my own birthday, but everyone celebrates the man whose face we never have seen," Ben said.

"Does everyone celebrate?" I asked.

"In France, Russia, Italy, the Netherlands, and many other countries," Ben said.

"The one who died on the cross?" Kyu asked.

"Oh, more than eighteen hundred years ago he was born and died," Ben said.

"So long ago? Where was he born?" I asked, thinking of the doll's play.

"I don't know, but I know that December 25 is Christmas. Jesus Christ didn't give me anything, not even a lemon," Ben said.

"But do you still celebrate Christmas?" I asked.

"I do just to be sociable. Well, it's just a custom," Ben said.

An officer passed by. We shut our mouths and pretended to work hard. The officer walked away.

"Do you believe Jesus is the Son of God?" I asked doggedly.

"When there are no more poor people in this world, I will believe in Jesus Christ. But as long as the captain and the officers behave badly, I don't believe it," Ben said and spat.

I was surprised. If God heard his words, what would God think about them? *But even the Japanese say, "Is there any Buddha or any gods?"* I began to like Ben because he was not a Christian. I thought most of the sailors on the *Eagle* were almost the same as Ben.

"Kyu, I thought everyone on the *Eagle* was Christian, but they are not. When we go back to Japan, we must tell them about Ben," I said in Japanese.

"But how about the worship on Sunday? Everyone sang the hymns. After the captain prays, they say, 'Amen.'" Kyu said in Japanese.

"That was only part of their job," I said and relaxed. I looked at the figurehead, which was a beautiful woman with a long robe. Her hands held eagle's feet. I remembered Yuki. *This must be Funadama-san! I am going to pray to this figurehead as Funadama-san.*

"By the way, the captain called you yesterday, didn't he?" Ben asked.

"Oh, yes," Kyu answered.

"Did the captain ask about me?" Ben asked sharply.

Kyu and I were bewildered.

"The captain asked only about Japan. Don't say anything else," Iwa-san warned Kyu and me.

"What did you say?" I asked. Then he asked the same question, repeating it slowly and clearly.

"No, the captain asked only about Japan," I calmly answered.

"What kind of things did he ask about?" Ben asked.

"Who governs Japan, the military, food, kimonos," I said.

"Is that all?" Ben asked.

"Yes." I felt I should tell the truth to Ben, but Iwa-san said that was forbidden.

"The captain is afraid of me," Ben said and laughed without a sound. "Because … " Ben tried to say something.

"I am finished polishing. Do you need any help?" Dad asked, standing by us.

"Dad, thanks. Take a break. You sit there and pretend to polish the floor," Ben continued. "Dad, there were so many rebellions before," Ben said.

"You really like revolt stories," Dad said.

"Dad is great. He led rebellions," Ben said.

"Don't say that!" Dad shook his head.

"It is true. Dad also fought with Napoleon," Ben said proudly.

"But sailors are always sailors," Dad said with a calm tone.

"Kenta, why are you smiling happily?" Ben asked.

I turned my eyes from the figurehead and looked at him.

"Well, you are guests. The Hudson Bay Company gave the captain a lot of money. Take it easy," Ben said with warm voice.

The watcher shouted from the mast, "Land, ho!"

The sailors and the officer were astir.

"Good, we will have this Christmas on land." Ben's voice was exuberant.

~ ~ ~ ~ ~

Strange trees. They are blooming upside down. I saw the coconut palm tree for the first time. In order to fumigate the ship, all sailors on the *Eagle* had to leave the ship. Periodically they fumigated the ship to kill insects or bacterium by dipping wood branches and leaves into tar and creating smoke with burning charcoal. Of course the cannons were covered. One day before fumigation, everyone left the *Eagle*. Hawaii was warm, so we could sleep on the beach with only one blanket.

"It is like heaven!" Kyu said.

Stars shone. There were fires on the beach. The sailors sat around the fires and sang, danced, and drank. The captain and upper officers stayed at the pastor's house or in the church building. But the lower officers watched the sailors. If someone escaped, it was their responsibility.

"We have to give thanks to Jesus' mother," Ben said.

"Why?" I asked.

"She gave birth to her son on this day," Ben said.

"Indeed. Fumigation on Christmas day. If Christmas had been yesterday, we wouldn't have had the party on land," Dad said.

"So, cheer for the Mother of Jesus Christ!" Ben said.

"But Ben, Jesus has his father, Joseph," a long-nosed man said.

"Joseph is not related to Jesus," Ben said.

"Jesus has no father?" the long-nosed man asked.

"His father is God," Ben stated.

"Oh, Ben. You are a true believer!" Dad said.

Everyone laughed.

~ ~ ~ ~ ~

Iwa-san was quiet. He must have been thinking about Japan.

"I miss Japan," Kyu said.

I nodded.

"Kenta, Kyu. Don't you want to escape into the mountains?" Iwa-san asked with a low voice.

"Escape to the mountains?" Kyu's eyes grew wide.

"If we catch a whaling ship, we will get back to Japan in two months. Then we can say we were on an uninhabited island. The Japanese officials will let us go home," Iwa-san said.

"That is a good idea. We are afraid of the Japanese officials, but if we were on an uninhabited island, they wouldn't think we had become Christian," I said.

"Kenta, do you agree?" Iwa-san asked.

"But will we able to catch a whaling ship easily?" Kyu hung back.

All of a sudden, officers appeared. We were shocked and shut our mouths.

~ ~ ~ ~ ~

When I entered the dining room, I was stupefied. A whole baked pig on a huge plate was set on the table on a white tablecloth. Many big candle flames fluttered and it was as if the pig were still breathing.

Cruel! I shut my eyes.

"He is Kenta," the captain introduced me to a tall man. We didn't even notice the captain was there, because the whole baked pig made such a strong impression on us. I opened my eyes and saw several people. The captain and two officers stood around the table. A tall man and a young beautiful woman smiled at me. The captain said they were Pastor Brown and his wife, Kay. After the greeting, we all sat down.

We didn't understand the word *pastor*. There was no pastor in Fort Vancouver.

"When I talked about you, Pastor Brown wanted to invite you for the dinner," Captain Wise explained. I had to say thanks, but I was still thinking about the whole baked pig. *I ate pork and beef many times, but they were all separate pieces of meat.* Now they placed the whole pig on the plate and cut it with knives. I saw they killed the cows or sheep at Fort Vancouver. I was shocked, but I had never seen a whole pig on the plate. *Why do they eat the whole pig? It is cruel.* I looked at Kyu. His eyes were still on the pig. We ate supper at the beach: salted pork, hard bread, butter, cheese, sugar, and rum. Compared to the sailor's supper, this dinner was a deluxe edition, with wine, soup, salad, and green peas. If there had been no whole baked pig, this room would have been pleasant.

"How old are you, Kenta?" the pastor's wife, Kay, asked.

"Sixteen," I answered. She was young, perhaps twenty. Her eyes were blue like the sky, and her blond hair was beautifully curled.

"Would you please eat the pig? It is tasty," she said.

Did this beautiful woman bake this pig? I wondered.

Then Pastor Brown said, "The whole baked pig is this island's specialty. The island people bake it and bring it to us once in a while."

She didn't bake this pig. I felt relieved. I shut my eyes again and thought, *Do I have to eat this pig?* I felt dizzy.

"Do Japanese people pray to God?" the pastor asked.

"Yes, we do," Iwa-san answered.

"What kind of gods?" the pastor asked.

"I don't know how to answer. Kenta you must answer," Iwa-san said.

"In Japan, there are many gods, such as Oise-san, Konpira-san, Oinari-san, Funadama-san," I said.

"I see. Is there Jesus Christ?" Pastor Brown asked.

When I heard *Jesus Christ*, I was scared. I shook my head. "If we pray to Jesus Christ, we will all be killed. Even our families," I said.

"Killed!" Kay's eyes grew wide.

"I see. Do you know any Christians who were killed?" the pastor asked.

I tilted my head.

"I haven't seen any, but Amakusa Shiro was a famous Christian. When I was a child, many Christians were punished. If the Japanese officials found a cross, they were all killed," Iwa-san said in Japanese, so I translated it.

"It is awful that Christians were persecuted," the pastor said with a sigh.

"Many missionaries were killed, but I pray for your country. When the time comes, the Japanese will accept Christianity," Kay said with a beautiful low voice.

"They don't know the Japanese officials. If we became Christian, we will be hanged by the neck or crucified, and our families will be killed," Kyu said in Japanese.

I was not going to put up with Christians entering my country. When they started talking about Christianity, I felt depressed. I was afraid of Christianity more than the whole baked pig.

"Are there any letters in Japan?" the pastor asked.

"Yes, there are kanji, which came from China, and hiragana and katakana, which the Japanese invented. They could write their names in kanji," the captain answered.

"Oh, what a great country!" Pastor Brown seemed fascinated. "How about music and musical instruments?"

"Yes, we have the bamboo flute, drums, koto, shamisen, biwa," I said.

"Bang, bang, this is the drum, and musical notes from bamboo flute," Kyu demonstrated.

"I see. How about an organ or piano?" Pastor Brown asked.

"No, we don't have those," Iwa-san answered.

"How about pictures or scriptures?" Pastor Brown asked.

"Yes, sumie—pictures with black ink, and also pictures with color," Iwa-san replied.

After the dinner, I wrote Japanese letters and Iwa-san drew a big shoji sliding door painted with flowers and a tiger. He also painted a kakejiku, a hanging picture scroll, and painted mountains.

"Beautiful. Japan is a wonderful country," the pastor said.

"I think so, too. These three men are well mannered. They must be men of character," the captain praised us. His face was gentle, different from when he was on the *Eagle*.

"Yes, there are letters, art, scriptures, and weaving looms. But one problem is that there are too many gods in Japan, just like Athens in Greece," Pastor Brown said, and everyone nodded.

"There is only one God. I believe that nobody has told them yet," Pastor Brown said.

"Yes, when we send them back to Japan, it will be a chance to spread the gospel," Captain Wise said.

"But the persecution is severe," Pastor Brown said.

"Yes, but they are intelligent people. If someone will translate the Bible into Japanese, they will find out the true God's love," Pastor Brown said.

"Yes, but it's impossible. I don't think I could read or write such a difficult language," Captain Wise said and shook his head and sighed, looking at the letters that we wrote on the papers.

"Do you think so? Nothing is impossible with God. I believe Japan is a wonderful country. Someday, they will accept Jesus Christ," Kay said.

As they spoke fast, I couldn't understand well; I just heard "Jesus Christ" many times. *Why do they talk about Jesus Christ? I don't like Christianity. I am scared. I don't want Christianity to enter my country!*

Iwa-san was still painting a ship, the *Takaramaru*.

That night, we stayed at the pastor's house. Iwa-san did not want to stay, but Kay said, "Iwa, you are a guest of England. I don't want you to sleep on the beach." Also, the pastor and the captain urged us to stay.

We lay on thin mats on the floor. The room was warm.

"Iwa-san," I said.

"What?" asked Iwa-san.

"It was painful when they asked about Japan," I said.

"Yes, indeed," Iwa-san said.

"I remembered each memory," I said.

"Oh, I did, too. I prefer to forget about Japan," Iwa-san said.

"Iwa-san. Do you still think about escaping to the mountains?" Kyu asked.

"We started talking; then the watchers appeared," Iwa-san said.

"I was scared as if my all blood froze," I said.

"Did the watchers spoil our talking?" Iwa-san asked and laughed slightly.

"Yes, they had guns. Even if we escaped to the mountains, they would find us sooner or later," I said.

"Oh, Kenta, did you change your mind?" Kyu asked and seemed relieved.

"Yes, if someone spoiled our conversation, it's an unlucky sign. What do you think, Iwa-san?" I asked.

"If I am alone, I will escape, even if I can't make it and I am the only one to die.

But I don't want you to die," Iwa-san said.

Kyu and I were silent. If Iwa-san were alone, he could go to Japan, riding on a whaling ship easily. But three of us would be noticed. If Iwa-san left us, we wouldn't know how to survive.

"I am sorry, Iwa-san. Once we thought we were going to escape in Cape Flattery, but we were saved. I feel the gods are telling us not to escape," I said.

"But we may be able to get back to Japan in two months from here. If we go back to the *Eagle*, it will take one year," Iwa-san said.

"If we want to escape, today is the best time," I said.

"I will check around," Iwa-san said and left the room.

We couldn't leave the pastor's house that night. Iwa-san tried to go outside, but the watcher asked him where he was going. He said, "Bathroom."

The next morning, we were shocked to see the church and the white cross on the roof.

"Oh, this must be a church. A pastor must be like a Christian monk," Iwa-san said.

"We stayed in the Christian church. We must not tell it to the Japanese officials," I said.

"Yes, this is a secret," Kyu said.

"Iwa-san, we must ask the captain," I suggested.

"That is a good idea. Kenta, you speak good English, so you must ask," Iwa-san said.

After the breakfast, we stood up from the chairs.

"Captain, I have to ask you a favor," Iwa-san said, and we knelt on the floor.

The captain, the officers, the pastor, and Kay were surprised.

"Please sit down on the chair. You must not bow to humans," the pastor said.

But we still knelt down.

"Captain, would you please let us go back to Japan? Please," I asked.

Pastor Brown let us sit on chairs and said, "Captain, please listen to them."

The captain nodded and asked, "You mean you want to leave the *Eagle*?"

"Yes. We want to get off the *Eagle* and go straight back to Japan," I said.

"Do you have any dissatisfaction with the *Eagle*?" Captain Wise asked kindly.

"No, but we want to go back to Japan as soon as possible. Iwa-san has old parents, a wife, and a baby. If he doesn't go home, they will have a hard life," I said.

"I see," Captain Wise said.

"Kyu and I have older parents. My father is sick. Kyu's and my sisters are still so young," I said.

"Oh, it's painful. I understand why they want to go home as soon as possible," Kay said with tears in her eyes.

"We have been away from Japan for two years. If we wait one more year, it's too long. Moreover, our country forbids Christianity. If the *Eagle* brings us to Japan, the Japanese officials will kill us," I said. I made a desperate effort. I tried to use as many as vocabulary words as I had learned. I wanted him to understand our feelings.

The captain folded his arms and listened. He said, "I understand your feelings well. As I am a sailor, I feel the same way you feel. But I made a promise to Dr. McLoughlin. I have to take you to London, you know. The whaling ship is not safe, and they have no power to negotiate with Japanese officials. If the whaling ship wrecked, you wouldn't ever go back to Japan. If you don't want to attend the morning worship, you don't have to. Make haste slowly," the captain said. He was touched by our feelings; his expression and voice were sincere.

~ ~ ~ ~ ~

We left Hawaii on the *Eagle*.

I felt I wouldn't see my family ever again. I remembered my father's thoughtful words, mother's warm smile, tiny Hana, and Yuki's beautiful eyes. Tears rolled down my cheeks.

"Kenta, are you crying?" Kyu asked.

"..."

"Kenta, the pastor and Kay, were nice people," Kyu said.

"Hmm ..."

"Kay cared for us," Kyu said.

"She must be like an angel," I said and wiped my tears with my arm.

"Yes, she understood our feelings. She came from England," Kyu said.

"She must be lonely. But how can she live on such a small island peacefully?" I asked.

"Indeed. Why did she come from England?" asked Kyu.

Pastor Brown said they came to this island to tell the gospel of Jesus Christ. Someday missionaries would go to Japan, too.

Why do they choose such a difficult way? If they live in their own country, their lives must be peaceful. The pastor's wife reminded me of Piko. What is she doing? I hope she has a happy marriage. But why did the pastor and his wife come to this country? The pastor's job is mysterious. It is hard to understand.

"The pastor and his wife were wonderful people," Kyu said.

"Yes, they were very kind to us," I said.

"Kenta, I can't understand," Kyu said.

"What?" I asked, looking at the island. I couldn't see the papaya trees or houses anymore. They were only black shadows on the dark sea.

"Kenta, why do Japanese officials forbid talk about Christianity?" Kyu asked.

"I don't know. Mr. Bacon, Dr. McLoughlin, Pastor Brown, and Kay are very nice people, as if they were gods or Buddha. If they believe in Jesus Christ, Christianity must be a good religion. I don't understand why Christians have to be crucified," I said.

"Yes, I heard that Christians drink human blood, but Dr. McLoughlin and Mr. Bacon didn't drink blood," Kyu said.

"Oh, they drink the red wine. It looks like blood. Maybe someone made a mistake," I said.

"Indeed. Red wine is like blood. It's stupid. Do the Japanese officials believe such things?" Kyu asked.

"I don't know," I said.

"But if Christianity is a good religion, why don't they introduce it into our country?" Kyu asked.

"The captain said if we didn't want to attend worship, we didn't have to. But in Japan, if we did not join the Buddhist temple, they would say we must be Christians and we would be killed," I said.

"That is the Japanese officials. If the Japanese officials command it, we have to obey. 'Aye, aye, sir,'" Kyu said.

"Aye, aye, sir … terrible," I said. We looked at each other and sighed.

"Something is wrong in this world. But why do we have to be afraid of the Japanese officials?" Kyu asked and tilted his head.

"They have the power to put us into jail. If they couldn't do it, we wouldn't be afraid of them. There are many more farmers and fishermen than Japanese officials," I said.

"Indeed. But this is the same as what Ben said," said Kyu.

"Yes, we are like Ben now. Only a few officers beat many sailors. Now I can understand Ben's feelings," I said.

The supper bell rang.

~ ~ ~ ~ ~

It was a hot and humid night. We couldn't sleep well.

"Iwa, let us sleep on the deck. It's too humid. It's bad for our health," Dad suggested.

"Thanks. I will bring Kenta and Kyu," Iwa-san said.

We slept on the deck once in a while. The wind blew and we felt much better in the hot humid night. We all brought our blankets and went to the deck. Ben and Dad were there. Some sailors snored.

I lay on the floor and listened to Ben and Dad's conversation.

"Dad, I thought I was going to escape to the mountains," Ben said.

"I see. I understand. When we went to Hawaii, everybody thought that way. The flowers bloomed, the birds flew, and the island was full of coconut trees. When I was in Hawaii before, I felt like escaping to the mountains, too," Dad said.

"Really, Dad? Why didn't you escape?" Ben asked.

"Poor people like us are always the same everywhere we live. Everywhere we go, we have to obey someone," Dad said.

"I see … it's true. There is Chief Kamehameha in Hawaii. I couldn't stand that there are noblemen on that island," Ben said.

"But, Ben, why didn't you escape?" Dad asked.

"I didn't want to part from you," Ben said.

"Really?" said Dad.

"Yes, if I escape, Dad will be punished because Dad and I are best friends," Ben said. "I knew Dad would be whipped. So I didn't escape."

"Ben, I don't mind taking a whipping for you," Dad said gently.

"I know. You are such a man. That is why I follow you," Ben said. "Dad, thanks. I am happy because you wouldn't mind being whipped for me. I appreciate it very much," Ben said. "Dad, please live a long life."

"Thanks, Ben. You do the same," Dad said.

I felt almost like crying. *Ben is right. If someone didn't mind being whipped for me, I could live happily. I don't mind dying for my father, my mother, Hana, and Yuki.*

I looked up to the crescent moon. The blue light streamed down to the cabin.

South Sea

In 1835, we had our third New Year on the *Eagle* since we sailed from Japan.

This year, Marconi invented the wire telegraphy machine. Of course, I didn't know anything about it.

The *Eagle* sailed to the southeast from Hawaii. We enjoyed looking at the huge rainbows. The red sunset dyed the sea as if it were blood, and sometimes a white fog surrounded us.

A month passed. It got hot as if there were two suns in the sky. Every time we walked on the deck with bare feet, we felt burned. Many of us lost our appetites.

"I feel crazy!" Kyu shouted.

Kyu and I became thinner, and our cheeks became sunken. I couldn't think. I felt like my brain flew away to the sky.

The *Eagle* was close to the equator. Iwa-san took us to the bathroom and gave us a shower with the sea water. But I lost consciousness and was gasping. We all waited for the squall. When the heavy raindrops hit the deck, we all got naked and stood under the squall. We opened our mouths and drank.

I was surprised at how they collected the rain. The sailors held a big sheet and directed the rain into a barrel.

After thirty minutes of the squall, the temperature dropped. The squall was our refreshment.

When the *Eagle* was below the equator, there was an equator festival. But nobody had the energy to dance or sing. We tied ropes to our bodies and swam in the sea. But after we came out of the sea, we got hotter and weaker.

"If we go to the south, it gets hotter," I murmured.

"Oh, no. That's not true," Ben said.

"Why?" I asked.

"Relax, kid. This is the hottest place in the world. From now on, it will get cold. We will go to the frozen south," Ben said.

I felt relieved.

Two months had passed since we left Hawaii. Sailing with two hundred sailors and the officers was not easy. Moreover, controlling the ship was much more difficult. The weather had changed. Some days were calm, and other days were as rough as a huge wave hitting the ship. The sailors had to climb to the high mast every day, opening and closing the sails. Even though there was a good wind, they didn't use the lightest sail on the top of the mast at night, so the sailors had to close the sail at night and open the sail in the morning.

The captain told us, "Take it easy. You are guests."

But Iwa-san said, "Do not behave like a spoiled child. When you have a chance to learn, grab the opportunity."

Iwa-san followed Dad and learned how to climb the mast. It was the most difficult and dangerous training. Kyu and I tried it, too. The sailors climbed to the high mast as if they were monkeys, but when I tried the first time, it was hard to move my arms and legs. I had to hold shrouds, the taut ropes running from a master head to the channels on the side of the ship. Then my feet were on ratlines, the small ropes that join the shrouds of the ship horizontally and serve as a way for the sailors to go aloft. Then I had to keep my body balanced and distribute my weight equally. In case the ratlines were cut off, I still held the shroud so I wouldn't fall off. Iwa-san was very good at it. He was a fast learner. All the sailors and the officers looked at Iwa-san with admiration.

Another important thing was to know which line connected to which sail. There were so many lines, and we had to learn which line we must pull in order to open a certain sail. Kyu and I were good at it.

Controlling the mast was most important, because if it were done wrong, someone working on the mast might die. A very careful man must be in charge of this job. Dad was the best skilled man to control it. I followed Dad and learned. When Dad touched the ropes, he changed into a very serious man. He tightened his lips while loosing the rope, and his eyes were fixed on the sailors on the mast. Dad got tense as if this were his first experience. He said to Kyu and me, "There are two important things. We must be skillful and we must not be careless."

I never forgot his words.

~ ~ ~ ~ ~

I felt cool as if it were the end of fall. I woke up. *Too calm.* I went to the deck. Iwa-san stood there and looked at the sea. "A dead calm," Iwa-san said.

A dead calm was much more dangerous than a storm for a sailing ship. Without wind, the *Eagle* wouldn't move. All the sails were like dead leaves.

"The wind is down!" Iwa-san shouted. Everyone created a stir.

Two days passed. The sea was as still as death. There were gray spots on the white sea. I felt I could walk on the sea. There was an unearthly silence.

We didn't know from which direction the wind would come, so the sailors opened the head yard and the after yard in order to prepare for the wind. But the sea was as dead as if it forgot to breathe.

"It is like the god of the wind died," I said.

"If god of the wind were to die, it would be terrible. Even though two hundred sailors might blow, they can't make wind. They can't spread the sails," Kyu said.

Everyone felt nervous.

The bell rang. It was a sign of an emergency meeting. Captain Wise must have felt the sailors' feelings. He must have been afraid of rebellion, so he wanted to turn the sailors' attention to something else.

All the sailors and the officers came on deck. Then Lieutenant Carter talked. I had met him at the pastor's house. He was a good speaker and praised Iwa-san's drawing. "You are a great artist," he had said and gave Iwa-san special food once in a while.

"There is the Juan Fernandez Island near here. Do you know this island?" Lieutenant Carter asked.

Several sailors nodded, but most of them were puzzled.

"I see. Some of you don't know it, but I think everyone must have heard the name Robinson Crusoe," Lieutenant Carter said.

A stir ran through the sailors. Iwa-san, Kyu, and I didn't know Robinson Crusoe.

Some of the sailors didn't know, either.

Robinson Crusoe was a story written by Daniel Defoe in 1719. Robinson Crusoe lived on an uninhabited island for twenty-four years. His only friend was a parrot, until he met a black man, an escaped prisoner. Crusoe named him Friday. When this book was published, the title was long: *The Life and Strange Surprising Adventure of Robinson Crusoe of York, Mariner.* Soon this book was translated into several languages. It was a very famous story, but still some sailors didn't know it.

Lieutenant Carter began, "It was a true story." He looked around and said, "It was not fiction. Alexander Selkirk was the model."

Some sailors whispered suspiciously.

Twenty-four years? My eyes grew wide. *I can't live on an uninhabited island alone for even one year.*

The *Eagle* had stopped in the middle of the ocean for only two days, but we had already lost our minds. Robinson Crusoe's story lifted our spirits. Lieutenant Carter was a good speaker, as if he were an actor. He spoke clearly, so we could understand. He imitated the wind, the thunder sounds, and the birds singing excellently. I felt Robinson Crusoe's loneliness. He used a hammer and made his house. I felt I wanted to help.

"There was pure water, goats, and vegetables," Lieutenant Carter said.

All the sailors were charmed by the story.

"Oh, goats. It was good," I murmured.

"Yeah, he had food at least," someone whispered.

"Robinson Crusoe taught words to the parrot. 'Everything is fine. You will be happier.' Robinson read the Bible every morning and night, and prayed. His three Bibles were worn out. He always gave thanks to God. His prayers supported him," Lieutenant Carter said. He talked passionately. But he didn't tell that Alexander Selkirk lived on the island only five years, from 1606 to 1611. Twenty-four years was much more dramatic as a story. But he never forgot to say, "Everybody, do you know why Alexander Selkirk had to stay on this island? It was not because of the storm, but because he was against the captain, so the captain left Alexander alone in this uninhabited island."

The story had ended. The sailors still looked at each other. They forgot they were on a dead calm sea.

"I see. I don't want to be Robinson Crusoe," a sailor said.

"I can't stand to live twenty-four years by myself," said another sailor.

"We must not go against the captain," many sailors said.

The sailors felt Robinson's loneliness. Moreover, this story was not fiction. The sailors felt touched and also scared.

"We have a break until noon," the deck officer commanded.

"The Juan Fernandez Island was near here," Ben and Dad came closer and said.

"It was a great sermon, wasn't it?" Ben asked. "If I were him, I would tell a much more interesting story, about William Bligh."

"Bligh? I see," Dad said, laughing.

"Please tell me," Kyu asked.

"This story is much more interesting than Robinson Crusoe. Dad knows it better. Dad, could you tell us?" Ben asked.

Dad nodded and began. "It was 1789. Now it is 1835. How long ago?" asked Dad.

"Forty-six years ago," I replied.

"I see, Kenta, you are good at math. Well, there was a ship, called *HMS Bounty*. Bligh was the only officer on this ship. He was a very greedy commanding lieutenant who cut down the sailors' food ration in order to save money for himself. He was a cruel tyrant," Dad said.

"He was a bad man! Of course the sailors got angry," Ben said.

"Yes, nobody wanted to be involved in a rebellion, but his subordinates pushed Bligh and his supporters away in his small boat. Nineteen people were in a twenty-three-foot launch, with four cutlasses, a pocket watch, and a sextant," Dad said.

"Where was it?" I asked.

"South Pacific. But they were given a little water, salted meat, and hard bread."

"They died, right?" I asked.

"The Bible says, 'God will give the sun and the rain to good and bad.' Bligh was an extremely tough man. He reached England in 1790," Dad said.

"It was surprising. If our captain were left alone on a small boat, he would not survive even one day," Ben said.

"Don't say that, Ben. No one could be like Bligh. He must have had storms, hunger, and Indian attacks. He overcame these troubles and came back to England.

Bligh was a very highly skilled sailor," Dad said.

"Oh! He survived?" I asked.

"Yes. Bligh was a greedy man, but he was an extremely powerful man both physically and spiritually. Later he became vice admiral of the Blue. The rebels were shocked, because Bligh rode a big ship and tried to catch them," Dad said.

"See, this story is much scarier than *Robinson Crusoe*, but of course, Captain Wise won't tell such a thing. If they had left the captain and the officers in the boat, they would have had no chance to survive," Ben said.

"Bligh was an excellent sailor. He is like Iwa-san," Kyu said.

"But Iwa-san is not greedy," I said.

Iwa-san was still looking at the dead calm.

~ ~ ~ ~ ~

After the dead calm, we experienced the most difficult sea, in Cape Horn, South America. We enjoyed looking at the Andes Mountains with snow, and then the sea became rough like an angry dragon. The wind mixed with snow hit our skin as if it were arrows. We wore thin cloth, made of tapa bark, under our clothes. The tapa Pastor Brown gave us kept us from being cold. But still the wind hit us like needles. The waves bubbled white. The *Eagle* was lifted to the top of the waves and then plunged to the bottom of the waves. The sail billowed in the wind and almost tore. Some sailors slipped down on the icy deck. The tide of Cape Horn moved back and forth from the Pacific Ocean to Atlantic Ocean. The wind blew in the same way. The *Eagle* ran fast as if it were a crazy horse.

Some sailors checked how much the sea water penetrated the ship; others sewed the sails.

"If you don't know the storms of Cape Horn, you are not yet a sailor," Ben said.

I thought we experienced a bad storm when we sailed with the *Takaramaru*, but Cape Horn's storm was one hundred times stronger than the storm I experienced. The waves occurred from the bottom of the sea.

The waves became calm. The bell rang. Everyone went to the deck.

"Open the sail!" the officer shouted.

The shrouds and the ratlines were frozen. The sailors climbed the icy shrouds without shoes or gloves. The sails were frozen as well. I felt it was a miracle that no one fell down into the sea. My hair was chilled like icicles; my breath was white as if I could catch it. My eyebrows, eyes, ears, and nose were all frozen. I had never known such a cold place. Even when I spat, the saliva changed to ice. When I thought I saw an island, it was a huge wave. I was terrified.

"Quiet this time," Ben said, smiling.

"Ah? Is it quiet?" I asked.

"One hundred years ago, Admiral Anson's ship was in a huge storm. A wave like a monster hit the ship and the handrails were broken, and people and things were thrown into the sea. The sail tore, but they had no time to change the sail. So what do you think he used instead of the sail?" Ben asked.

We tilted our heads. *Is there anything else instead of the sail?*

"Sailors!" Iwa-san said.

"Oh, he ordered the sailors cling to the shrouds. The wind mixed with snow blew," Ben said.

"Wow! The sailors must have been blown away," Kyu said.

"Only one sailor blew away. It was a mysterious and famous story in England," Ben said.

I imagined that many sailors held the frozen shrouds in the storm. I was shivering. I wondered if Dr. McLoughlin saved us from the Cape Indians and tried to send us back to Japan because Bligh and Anson were also Englishmen.

"Iwa-san. This is like a boiling pot in hell. Last night I was wondering to which gods I must pray," Kyu said.

"I don't know. But I feel the world is huge. Many countries have different ideas, thoughts, and religions," Iwa-san said.

"I see," Kyu said.

"There is only one sun. I think there is only one God. I feel that way," Iwa-san said.

LONDON

The *Eagle* sailed down the Thames River. Heavy fogs surrounded us. Other ships brushed past. A ship with smoke jumped into view.

"There is no sail! It must be a steam ship," Iwa-san said.

It shocked us. The ship was made of black iron, and the burning charcoal was the fuel. Another steam ship that had sails passed by.

We thought the *Takaramaru* with one mast was the largest ship. Then we saw the *Eagle* with three masts. Now we saw the steam ship. Our jaws dropped and we sighed.

"England is a great country," I said.

"Don't be too surprised. I heard there are steam carts running on two rails. The cart runs with a whistle. They can carry many people and things. The steam cart can run thirty miles per hour," Iwa-san said.

"In Japan, we use cows or horses to carry people and things on the land. I wish I could see the miracle cart," I said.

I thought it must be interesting to see the sights in London. But the Thames River was stinky. I heard that all the waste of London's citizens came into the river. I was disappointed with the river. In Japan, most of the rivers were pure and beautiful. We could swim and catch fresh fish.

Finally, the *Eagle* reached London. Many sailors left the ship, but we stayed on the ship with the captain and a few officers.

"Hope you can get back to Japan," Ben said.

"I learned about Japan, looking at three of you, conscientious, hard-working, and mild tempered. Good luck," Dad said and left the *Eagle* with Ben. We watched their backs. *We will never see them again.* I almost felt like crying.

"I like Ben," I said.

"Yes, Dad is a nice man, too," Kyu said.

"What kind of ship will we have next?" Kyu asked.

"It may be a steam ship," Iwa-san said teasingly.

~~~~~

After three days, the fog cleared up.

"What is that?" We saw the London Tower in the distance. It was different from the Japanese castle. It was made of stone and had a huge clock on the tower. I also saw three-story houses made of wood. The sailors were going in and out, so they must be the sailors' inns. There were many large barrels of beer in front of these houses.

The captain was still looking for a ship for us.

Dr. McLoughlin was planning to open a port with Japan, so he wanted us to see England. Even though the English government didn't agree with Dr. McLoughlin's opinion, he felt it would be a good benefit to let us see England. But when we arrived in London, the English government's policy was determined.

A few years ago, England was interest in trading with Japan, but they lost interest.

England imported tea from China and had an enormous benefit, because Europeans started to drink the tea. England wanted to export woolen goods, but China didn't buy them. English silver was spent in China. The English government took measures to deal with these situations. Dr. McLoughlin's idea was praised as humanitarian, but he let the Hudson Bay Company pay the expense. The Hudson Bay Company warned him; nevertheless, the Hudson Bay Company had to return us to Japan. These things I learned later.

"Beautiful day today. I want to take you to see London, but we don't have the permit from the government, yet. But I think they will give you permission soon," the captain said.

"Thank you, sir." We bowed deeply.

England had the East India Company in Macao. The East India Company used to have a monopoly on trade power during the Qing Dynasty. But America gained and England lost the monopoly; therefore, fewer ships went to Macao.

"We have to submit an official document. Please sign your names," the captain said and placed the document on the desk.

Iwa-san wrote with a feather pen. "On October 10, 1832, we left

Atsuta, Japan …" After he finished writing, he wrote his name in katakana. Kyu and I signed in kanji. (This official document is still kept by the English Ministry of Foreign Office.)

"You came from far away, and you also worked hard. You are the first Japanese to enter our country," Captain Wise said, smiling and he told a story.

In 1803, a Russian warship came to London. Four Japanese who reached Russia in 1793 were on board, but English officials did not allowed them to land.

We were all surprised to hear the four Japanese were kept in Russia and came to England.

The seagulls cried noisily.

We stayed on the *Eagle*. We were getting used to the bad smell on the river.

"I want to eat fresh sashimi." I sighed.

"Yes, hot rice, miso, sashimi, soy sauce, wasabi. I am tired of salted meat and hard bread," Kyu said.

"I miss manju." I swallowed saliva.

Then Iwa-san came running. "The captain found a ship. We will be leaving the *Eagle* in two days." His voice vibrated.

"Really!" Kyu and I shouted; we both clapped our hands.

"But the ship goes by way of Macao. Then we have to find another ship, going back to Japan. The Hudson Bay Company will pay all the expenses. We will visit London tomorrow. We better go to sleep early tonight," Iwa-san said.

The ship only goes to Macao? Can we go back to Japan? I looked at the dark sea. I was uneasy.

~ ~ ~ ~ ~

London was clear on that day. We changed to suits, ties, and silk hats and rode in a carriage and pair with Lieutenant Carter. Two horses shook their heads and walked slowly. We were all excited, looking around from the carriage. The sailing ships came and went on the Thames River. There were many inns for sailors and storage buildings. We didn't see many houses. I felt the warm June breeze. The big elm trees reminded us of Fort Vancouver.

"Very good streets," Kyu said. We could see the stone pavement roads everywhere.

"Yes, but the roads were in terrible condition before," Lieutenant Carter said.

"Really!" We were surprised.

"That is right. The horses' legs buried in the dirt, and carriages fell over all the time," the coachman said.

"Yes, George II and his queen tried to commute from the Windsor castle to another castle. It was only a few miles, but they were not able to reach it in a day. The carriage fell over, and the coachman or guests broke their necks or legs; such things were daily matters," Lieutenant Carter said.

"Indeed, then they put boards on the road and let the horses walk on the boards," the coachman said.

"We have arrived at the London Tower. It is a huge, strongly made building."

"Is this the king's castle?" I asked.

"It was before," Lieutenant Carter said and looked at the gray tower. He bit his lip.

"Before? Who is living there now?" I asked.

"Political offenders," Lieutenant Carter said.

We didn't know the meaning of *political offenders*. We all tilted our heads.

"This is jail for people who were against the government," Lieutenant Carter said.

"Jail!" I shouted, raising my eyebrows.

We looked at the solemn tower.

"Very bad men go there?" I asked.

I felt uneasy after I heard that it was the jail. There were guards with black and red uniforms with swords. They stood with stern faces.

"Well, my best friend's father was killed here last year," Lieutenant Carter said; his eyes became dark like the midnight sea.

We looked at him silently.

"He was a great nobleman. Everyone respected him. Good and bad are killed in this tower," Lieutenant Carter said.

We couldn't understand what his words meant. He looked at the London Tower with angry eyes.

"There is a gate. The noblemen or political offenders are carried in by ship, but once they go in, they can't come out," Lieutenant Carter said.

"Why can't they come out?" I asked.

"They are beheaded with axes," Lieutenant Carter said and pretended to cut his neck with his hand.

I felt goose bumps. "Why was a nice man killed?" I asked.

"If someone criticizes it, the government wants to kill that person. Someone's comment is important. By the way, King Henry VIII beheaded two of his queens in this tower. Do you know why?" Lieutenant Carter asked.

"Well … ?" I tilted my head.

"They must have had affairs," Kyu said.

"One of them had affairs. This is a long story to tell. His first queen, Katharine of Aragon, couldn't have a son. She became pregnant almost twenty times, but only one princess, Mary, survived. The Catholic Church didn't allow them to divorce, so King Henry made his own church and divorced his first wife. They had been married more than twenty years. She was getting older, so King Henry wanted to marry a younger woman to have a son as his heir," Lieutenant Carter said.

"Hmm … "

"Then he married Anne Boleyn. She became pregnant a few times, but only one princess survived. Anne was the mother of Queen Elizabeth I. Henry wanted to have a third wife. So he made the false accusation of adultery, and he beheaded his second queen, Anne. His third wife, Jane Seymour, had a son, Prince Edward. Jane was a very obedient woman and completely submissive to the king. Every time she received a letter from the king, she knelt and bowed before she read it. The king loved her very much, but Queen Jane died right after she had her son. Then he married a German princess, Anne of Cleves, but he lost interest after he met her, so he divorced her; they remained like a brother and a sister. Then he married young, beautiful Katharine Howard, but she was disappointed. She thought the king was just a fat old man. She was in love with a young, handsome soldier, so she was beheaded. Then he married his sixth wife, Katharine Parr. She was a very beautiful lady, like a lily in the valley, and also religious. She took good care of the king's children; she also wrote Christian devotional books. Because of these books, she was sent to jail by a bad priest, but King Henry showed her mercy. She survived. After the king died, she inherited enormous wealth and became a very wealthy woman in England. But King Henry's wives were always afraid of not having a son," Lieutenant Carter said.

"Oh, the king of England was a bad man," Kyu groaned.

"Oh, no, not all the kings were bad. Some kings were good. But once a human has power, they tend to make big mistakes," Lieutenant Carter said.

Iwa-san nodded. "Yes, the Japanese officials are the same way. Many innocent people were killed, including Christians. I really don't understand why the Japanese officials kill all Christians," Iwa-san said in Japanese. So I translated it in English to Lieutenant Carter.

"Your country has tremendous government officials," Lieutenant Carter said.

The carriage moved on. Most of the houses were made with stones. I looked at the people on the street. In Japan, curly hair was not considered beautiful, but most of the women had curly hair in London. The people looked at us curiously.

Our carriage arrived at a huge building.

"Westminster Abbey is the one of London's oldest and best known churches. The church's huge tower is 365 feet above the ground. It is made of stone without any nails," Lieutenant Carter explained.

In Japan, they make the castles or the temples of wood without nails. But Westminster Abbey was too huge. I wondered how they could build like that. I was speechless.

"In 1066, William, the conqueror was crowned king in Westminster Abbey. The church has been added to and remodeled over the centuries, but some of its present architecture dates from the year 1200," Lieutenant Carter said.

How solemn! Many carpenters must have lost their lives. It had an extremely high ceiling; huge pillars stood on both sides. All of the pillars were made of stones. The ceiling was an arch shape as if I were looking at the bottom of the valley. I saw the many beautiful stained-glass windows. I was also shocked that they made them more than one thousand years ago. The colors were not painted on the glass; they used colorful glass and made beautiful figures of people, flowers, and birds. My jaw dropped, and I stood there as if I had become a stone statue.

"This kind of building is called Gothic architecture. Gothic came with the stained glass," Lieutenant Carter explained with a smile.

In front of the center, there was a gold cross and statues of saints.

"This must be a Christian temple," Iwa-san said.

"Yes, there are many crosses here," Lieutenant Carter said.

"The English sincerely care about Jesus Christ. If the Japanese officials saw this temple, what would they say?" I asked.

After I entered this church, I felt holy. If I stayed there longer, my heart would be pure like the spring water. I thought this must be a god's house.

"Almost all the country's monarchs have been crowned king in Westminster Abbey. Also, kings and queens, many politicians, professors, and writers were buried here, too. Oh, Shakespeare, too," Lieutenant Carter said.

"Shakespeare?" We were all puzzled.

"Don't you know him? He died two hundred years ago. He was a poet and playwright. He wrote thirty-seven plays, such as *Hamlet*, *Macbeth*, *Romeo and Juliet* ... I am honored to have been born in England, the same country with Shakespeare. Iwa-san, if you were English, you would be buried here, also. You are a great artist. Your paintings are unique," Lieutenant Carter praised Iwa-san.

Iwa-san smiled.

"Well, you speak English very well," Lieutenant Carter said.

"Yes, Mr. Bacon taught us. We attended Dr. McLoughlin's school, too. Mr. Bacon was an excellent teacher. At first, he taught us the nouns, things that we use daily, such as cup, plate, fork, spoon, etc. If we couldn't see something, he drew the pictures. When he taught us verbs, he imitated by gestures, such as write, dig, wipe, etc. Then we repeated it again and again," I explained.

"I see; you had intensive training," Lieutenant Carter said admiringly.

"Everything is different from Japan. Food, clothes, houses, words, the color of eyes, hair, and skin," Kyu said.

"Indeed; the god is different, too." I sighed.

"But we have the same hearts. We could understand Dr. McLoughlin and Mr. Bacon," Iwa-san said.

Kyu and I agreed with Iwa-san.

"London is a great city," I said.

"Hmm ... but London became clean only after a big fire in 1666. Before that, one hundred thousand people died from plague, which was a disease caused by rats. At that time, four hundred thousand citizens lived in London. All the citizens might have died, but the big fire happened, and it continued for four days. The entire rat population was killed. So London survived," Lieutenant Carter said.

I learned many things in London. Westminster Abbey was extremely beautiful, but I also saw the poor. I heard that nine-year-old children worked outside the home. I remembered my tiny sister, Hana. Ben, Dad, and the sailors on the *Eagle* were poor as well. I was also surprised that some houses were built along curving streets. I had never seen these kinds of skills in Japan.

We also visited the Hudson Bay Company. It was a small three-story building, but it had a distinctive character. There were many furs in the basement.

We were invited for dinner at the Hudson Bay Company. The beefsteak and the soup were very tasty. The first time I ate meat, I had goose bumps, but now I enjoyed eating meat. I felt I was not Japanese anymore.

In June, the sun rose before 3:00 am in London. At 6:00 am, we left the *Eagle* and rode on another ship, the *Cambridge*, a 532-ton cargo ship. There were seventy crew members and thirty passengers. The ship was not a warship, but there were some cannons, in case of pirate attack. There were also two women passengers. Captain Kid, with gentle eyes and a brown mustache, welcomed us.

I thought nobody would see us off, but Ben and Dad came.

"Good luck," Dad said.

"We will go to Japan someday," Ben said.

"Good-bye!" We waved.

The ship parted from the quay.

"Sayonara," Kyu shouted.

The seagulls cried and flew around the ship.

"Sayonara ..."

Soon, London disappeared from sight.

Part 3 (1835–1837)

SAIL AGAIN

Our new ship, the *Cambridge*, passed the Strait of Dover, which was calm as a sleeping baby. Two women, one Captain Kid's wife and the other a merchant's wife, sailed with us. Kyu was always excited, looking at them, but I felt they were for the Western men. I had no attraction to these two women. Yuki was still my only girl. *Is she married to someone else?* I felt sad, but I still couldn't forget her.

The supper was a little bit better than on the *Eagle*. The sailors still ate salted meat and dried bread, but there were vegetables, too. Most of the guests brought their own food. I saw sheep, chickens, pigs, and even cows. Several people cooked eggs and drank coffee or wine. *They must be rich.* Of course some of them were poor, but we were still lucky. The Hudson Bay Company paid all our expenses.

In order to sail on this ship, passengers had to give expensive gifts or money to the ship owner or to the captain. Most of the guests were noblemen, merchants, or elite businessmen, and their families. But still we had to sleep on the floor in the cargo cabin. It was a huge cabin with a very high ceiling, so they could carry a lot of cargo. There were no guest rooms, so everyone had to sleep on the floor, except Captain Kid and a few officers.

"Food on the *Takaramaru* was much better than on the *Cambridge*. We all ate the same thing," Kyu said.

I nodded and asked, "When will we be arriving in Macao, Iwa-san?"

"I don't know anything about tomorrow," Iwa-san said with a gloomy voice.

Yes, Iwa-san was right. We thought we were all going home safely, but we had spent the New Year away from Japan three times. We went to North America, Cape Horn, the equator, and London. We rode a warship and now we were on a cargo ship.

"But we are still lucky," I said.

"Why?" asked Kyu.

"When we left Atsuta, we were fourteen men, but eleven died and only three are left. We were saved from the Cape Indians. Also the Hudson Bay Company pays all our expenses. We are survivors," I said.

"That is right, Kenta. We don't know what will happen tomorrow, but there are not only bad things are waiting for us," Kyu said, smiling.

It was the first Sunday morning on the *Cambridge*. The cow cried, "Moo," as if the cow joined the worship. I thought that worship was held only on the *Eagle*, but I was wrong. Did all ships have a worship service? I thought we wouldn't be able to run away from Christianity until we got back to Japan. The pastor's message was much clearer and easier to understand than that of the captain of the *Eagle*. Pastor Jones sailed on the *Cambridge* at his own expense in order to pray and to encourage the people in the ship.

The pastor read the Bible, "The Jewish leaders and Pharisees brought out a woman caught in adultery and placed her in front of the staring crowd. 'Teacher,' they said to Jesus, 'this woman was caught in the very act of adultery. Moses's law says to kill her. What about it?' They were trying to trap him into saying something they could use against him, but Jesus stooped down and wrote in the dust with his finger." The pastor continued, "Jesus always said to forgive seven times seventy, which means we must forgive unlimited times. If you were Jesus, what would you do? Obeying God's law was extremely important to the Jewish people. There were so many rules, such as the women couldn't cook on the seventh day. One Jewish town was attacked on the seventh day. So they didn't fight, and they lost. For them, obeying God's law was much more important than winning." The pastor looked around at us. Then Pastor Jones started reading the Bible again.

"When they kept on questioning him, he straightened up and said to them, 'If any one of you is without sin, let him be the first to throw a stone at her.' Again he stooped down and wrote on the ground. At this, those who heard began to go away one at a time, the older ones first, until only Jesus was left, with the woman still standing there. Jesus straightened up and asked her, 'Woman, where are they? Has no one condemned you?' 'No one sir,' she said. 'Neither do I condemn you,' Jesus declared, 'Go now and leave your life of sin.'"

The pastor's voice became strict. "Everyone has sins. Nobody is perfect. I am a sinner, and so are the rich, the poor, the noblemen, the farmers, and even a king, too. Everyone is a sinner as long as he or she is a human. So no one could stone her. Jesus told these men, but also he told all people in the world. Yes, he said to you, each one is a sinner." The pastor's voice had dignity. Many people were silent awhile.

"It was a great sermon! Jesus Christ was an admirable man. But it's very difficult to follow his teachings," Iwa-san said.

I agreed with Iwa-san. "Pastor Jones is a professional. A good speaker! It was easy to understand and it was an excellent story," I said.

Kyu didn't listen to the sermon carefully. He had watched the two women. Some snored or others looked at the sea. It was different from the *Eagle*, so even though some didn't listen to the message carefully, nobody was blamed.

"The pastor said that the rich, poor, noblemen, farmers, and kings are all sinners," I said.

"But I don't steal or kill anyone," Kyu complained.

"But Pastor Jones said, 'Thinking only of your own benefit is a sin.' Everyone thinks of himself; therefore, we are all sinners," Iwa-san said.

"But, Iwa-san, there are some noblemen on this ship, but the pastor said clearly, even the noblemen were sinners," I said.

"I think so, too. I realized that some noblemen nodded, too," Iwa-san said.

"Really? But if the English king is here, he must be angry," I said.

"Well, I don't think the king would be angry at his message. If he got angry, he could prohibit Christianity, but he doesn't. So he must not get angry," said Iwa-san.

"Well, the English king has a broader mind than the Japanese officials. The Japanese officials would put the pastor in the jail if he said everyone is a sinner," I said.

"Kenta, Kyu, I agree with the pastor's words. If we take off our clothes, the rich and the poor are the same," Iwa-san said.

"But, Iwa-san …" I said.

"We are born into a poor family or rich family. That is the only difference," Iwa-san insisted.

"If the samurai or the shogun heard such things, there would be big problems," Kyu said and shrugged.

The sea became light blue. The sun was so bright that I was dazzled.

THE SLAVE ISLAND

The *Cambridge* passed between Africa and Cape Verde. There was a small island to the left side. Pastor Jones looked at the island. He seemed strained and bowed then prayed.

"What is he praying for?" Kyu asked.

"Indeed. I am interested in what he is praying for," the captain's wife, Ria, stood near us with several guests.

"Praying is the pastor's business. So he must have been praying for our safe trip," a short, fat man with a pipe said.

"Maybe he is praying for his family," a tall, skinny man said.

"If he is just praying for his family or our journey's safety; he is not a different man from us," a bald man who always walked proudly said and laughed sarcastically.

"Then what should he pray for?" a short, fat man asked.

"I don't know, but I hope he is different from a layman," the bald man said.

"Well, shall we bet one pack of tobacco? The pastor prays for his family or he prays for completely different matters," the short, fat man suggested, wiping his forehead with a white handkerchief.

The men loved to gamble, especially when they became bored. They bet on many things, such as the weather.

"That is fun. I will bet that he is praying about completely different matters," the bald man said.

The rest of them bet on other matters.

They waited for him to finish praying. Then Ria and all the men got closer to the pastor.

"Kenta, let's go see," Kyu said, pulling my arm.

I nodded; then I invited Iwa-san, too. He followed us. We had not seen Pastor Jones praying alone on the deck since the *Cambridge* left London.

"Pastor Jones, what did you pray for?" Ria asked him innocently.

"That is a famous island, Goa," the pastor said, and pointed to the island.

"Oh!" all the men and Ria shouted.

There was a low hill, a featureless island.

"Are there any interesting things there?" I asked.

"Interesting things?" Pastor Jones talked slowly as if we were his elementary school students. "That island is a frightening place."

"Frightening? Are there any ghosts?" Kyu asked.

"It was much worse than ghosts. It was a slave-trading island. Since the seventeenth century, many slaves were killed on that small island," Pastor Jones said and he narrowed his eyes.

Goa Island, one thousand feet by three hundred feet, was found by the Portuguese in 1444. The Dutch, English, and French fought for this small island. Finally, the island became France's territory in 1802.

There was an entrance toward the sea. The slaves went in there and came out to be sold to many countries. From 1400 to 1800, Goa Island was slave territory. About 30 million slaves were sold. Most of the slave merchants were Arabians and West Europeans, but even the Africans joined the slave hunting. Moreover, some African chiefs sold their own people in order to earn money.

"Pastor Jones, did you pray for the slaves?" Ria asked.

"Yes, I also asked forgiveness of the Caucasian's sin," he said and walked away from the cabin.

"Well, I won the bet. Please give me the tobacco," the bald man said and stretched out his hand.

Two men gave him their tobacco cases.

"Well, if I must lose a tobacco case, at least it is in order to make amends for our sins," a tall, skinny man said.

"What did you say?" a very wealthy merchant asked.

"Did I say something wrong?" asked the tall, skinny man.

"You said to make amends for our sins. In England, it is prohibited to have slaves any longer," the very wealthy merchant said.

"I see. You are fabulously rich. Of course rich people had a lot of slaves. That's a shame," the tall, skinny man said and laughed.

"Why do you laugh? It was an order from the British royal families, so I obeyed. But I want to send the member of the assembly who passed the slave law to the London Tower," the wealthy merchant said.

"Really?" asked the tall skinny man.

"You know we used slaves for years. We paid for them. The slaves were our possessions," the wealthy merchant said.

"Yes, yes. The slave system existed before Jesus Christ was born. I don't think any countries without slaves exist," the bald man said.

"Well, is it a good thing if humans trade humans?" the tall, skinny man asked.

"Of course not. But Aristotle said slaves were living tools. Others said they were tools with a voice. The slaves were necessary for our society. It was low cost, so our society became prosperous. Not only England, but also France, Italy, Spain, the Netherlands, and many countries gained glory using slaves," the wealthy merchant said.

"How about the slaves' happiness?" the tall, skinny man asked.

"The slaves' happiness? Don't make jokes. Do we think of happiness of cows or sheep when we eat them?" the wealthy merchant replied.

"Wow! I am shocked. You think a human and an animal are the same. You are like *the Merchant of Venice*," the tall, skinny man yelled.

"Don't say that! I am not greedy like *The Merchant of Venice*," the wealthy merchant said.

"Indeed, indeed. You are not greedy," the young man said and gave a cynical smile. "Of course, you are neither greedy nor cruel. You are respected as a wealthy merchant. Your heart didn't ache even when the slaves stood on the block. The buyers checked them as if they were pigs or sheep. Your only interest was how to earn money. I have to take my hat off for your brave heart. Oh, I need a hundred hats in order to take them off."

"Earning money is the merchant's mission. Everything is about money. If we have money, we can buy not only women, but also their heart," the wealthy merchant said.

"Oh, I didn't know that. There is no almighty except God. Is your god made of gold?" the tall, skinny man asked.

The merchant couldn't answer.

"You are such a believer. People can't buy everything. One thing we can't buy is our heart and another is slaves," the tall, skinny man said.

"Oh, this is a great sermon. Jesus Christ must be crying. Listen, everyone, this young man will be an excellent pastor. A person who lives on his parents' money can't understand how the slaves were important in the world," the wealthy merchant said.

"Oh, I don't understand it. But anyway, more English thought like me than like you; therefore, the slave system is prohibited in England," the tall, skinny man said.

"What?" the merchant asked; his face became red and he raised his fist.

Suddenly, Ria spoke. "Well, gentlemen. It is charming when men argue." Her cheerful voice calmed them down. "It was a wonderful show. I was not expecting such a dramatic play while looking upon Goa Island. Who was the director of this drama?" Ria's voice was joyful, and she smiled beautifully.

The guests were wondering what was going on and clapped their hands.

The merchant said, "I have one more word." He grunted to the young man and said with a gesture, "You must be appreciating that there is no Hyde Park." (Hyde Park was used for dueling in London.)

"Oh sure. I will praise your shiny gold god." The tall, skinny man shrugged his shoulders.

"Well, it was an excellent end. I want to ask you for an encore, but we have not enough time. We have to prepare for supper soon," Ria said.

The guests clapped their hands again and left the deck.

"I thought they would fight; then they become calm. Shout and then settle down. We can't do such things," Kyu said. "Which one was wrong?"

"I didn't understand well, but the young man said trading the slaves was bad," I answered.

We were slaves in Cape Flattery. Ah-Dank whipped us like a cow or a horse. But some slaves were much more miserable. A mother and her children were sold separately.

"Kenta, we were slaves of the Indians. Then Dr. McLoughlin saved us and he didn't treat us as slaves. But there were slaves in England. I can't understand it," Kyu said.

"Kyu is right. The pastor said that humans are all the same. Many people nodded, even the wealthy merchant. I agree with the pastor's words. We shouldn't sell or buy humans. Humans are different from cows or elephants. In Japan, some parents didn't sell their sons, but they sold their daughters. Many Japanese thought women were on a lower level than men. I felt the English women were treated better than the

Japanese women. But still the English traded other countries' people. I hoped they showed kindness just as they treated us," Iwa-san said.

"Kyu, the pastor said that humans are all the same but everyone didn't understand it yet. That was the reason he taught us. If everyone really understood it, the pastor wouldn't have to say, 'A king, the rich, and the poor are the same,'" I said.

"They must know the logic, but they don't understand it in their hearts," Iwa-san said.

After the supper, I asked Pastor Jones, "Pastor, are slaves and the English the same?"

The pastor looked at me gently and said, "It is a very good question. We are all the same in front of God."

"Why then did they buy or sell slaves?" I asked.

"It is shameful. Many people just listen to the message as one of the Bible's stories," Pastor Jones answered; his eyes became dark.

I watched the Ivory Coast, the Golden Coast, and the Slave Coast.

When we heard about elephants, we couldn't figure it out. They said the elephant's ivory was eleven or twelve feet long. Then how big was the elephant? Someone drew a picture for us. We all felt the elephant was a mysterious animal with a long nose. A huge amount of ivory was exported from that small Ivory Island. The island people hid the ivory for many centuries.

I looked at the Slave Coast again. I heard that the buyers checked the slaves' teeth to see if there were any cavities, touched their muscles, and estimated how much they could lift. Then the buyer tried to cut down the price. The slaves couldn't get any money. They were just items for sale, like fish or vegetables.

A squall came. The guests shouted for joy. The Slave Coast disappeared from my sight.

"Cape Town is hard to sail, like Cape Horn," I heard from a sailor. But the color of the sea around Cape Town was as beautiful as the sea of heaven.

"I have never experienced such calm in Cape Town," Captain Kid said.

"Maybe because the special Japanese are on board," the people said.

The sea of Cape Town was so huge it seemed as if we could look at the end of the world.

~~~~~

"Oh, rain will come!" Kyu said. Everyone was so glad when we saw the thunderclouds and heard a roll of distant thunder. The *Cambridge* sailed north and passed by the Indian Ocean. We were going to pass the equator for the fourth time.

We saw the white sails a mile away for a few days.

"Pirate ship, isn't it?" Kyu's voice sound serious.

"What is that?" I asked.

There was a black cloud hanging from the towering thundercloud.

"It is like an elephant's nose," Kyu said.

"A whirlwind!" someone shouted.

Everyone's face became pale.

"If it reaches us, we will all die!" a sailor screamed.

"Turn the ship to the left!" Captain Kid ordered.

The whirlwind came closer like a running tiger.

"Oh!" everyone shouted.

The black cloud covered the ship that sailed one mile ahead of us. Then the whirlpool changed to a column of water that rose around sixty feet; then it turned to the right. The next moment, the column of water was gone. The thunder still roared.

"The ship is gone!" the sailor shouted from the mast.

I didn't know what it meant.

"The ship was dragged in," Iwa-san said.

"What?" I couldn't believe it. The ship was dragged into the whirlwind. Now I saw it was a much more dangerous thing than the storm. *Funadama-san, help me!* Many people prayed to Jesus Christ. They shouted, cried, or moaned. Big raindrops fell on the deck. *How long will this last?*

The rain and the thunder stopped. We saw the blue sky and the clouds ran far away. A big fish was on the deck. Kyu held it, and some guests looked at him.

It was a miracle. The ship that sailed a mile away was destroyed and the *Cambridge* was saved. I felt it was an undeniable fact.

MACAO

In December 1835, the *Cambridge* reached Macao. All the guests left the *Cambridge* except Iwa-san, Kyu, and I. The captain would look for our ship. Our hearts were full of joy. *We can go back to Japan soon!* Macao was a beautiful cape with seven hills and a small six-square-mile island. In 1557, the Portuguese migrated there.

Five days after we arrived in Macao, Captain Kid called us. *Did he find our ship?* But Iwa-san didn't think so. When we went to the captain's room, a woman was waiting for us. She was tall, with blue eyes and blond hair. Her skin was beautiful without any makeup.

"It's difficult to find a ship. It takes a while, so this lady is going to take care of you until we find a ship to Japan," Captain Kid said with a smile.

She was Mrs. Gutzlaff, a missionary's wife. We were all disappointed, but we had no choice. We bowed deeply.

"Mr. Gutzlaff is a genius with the written word. He can understand twenty languages," the captain said.

"Twenty!" Kyu said, rolling his eyes.

"Yes, he is German. He is very interested in Japan. He wants to learn Japanese," Captain Kid said.

Mrs. Gutzlaff smiled at us. Her eyes were warm and strong.

We followed Mrs. Gutzlaff. While we walked in the town, we saw Chinese men with pigtails. Their clothes were baggy. A salesman walked by with a carrying pole. When we saw the chrysanthemums on the street, we shouted with joy. They reminded us of Japan.

Soon we came to the housing area. There were flower pots by the bay windows that were similar to the houses in England.

Portuguese, English, American, Dutch and other foreigners lived in Macao.

Soon we arrived at Mr. Gutzlaff's house. His house was between a park and the museum. A smiling man dressed in Chinese clothes stood under the huge linden tree.

"He is my husband." Mrs. Gutzlaff introduced him. We bowed deeply. Mr. Gutzlaff extended his hand, so everyone shook hands with him.

They took us into a house. It was a clean-looking stone house. There were three rooms upstairs and three rooms downstairs.

"You can use this house just like your home. Our house is next door. Once in a while, guests come to stay here," Mrs. Gutzlaff said gently and left.

When can we go back to Japan? I sighed. I felt we had lost contact with the Hudson Bay Company.

We ate dinner at their house. The Cantonese food was excellent. We were all happy eating vegetables: carrots, daikons, green onions. It reminded me of the garden in my home town, and my mother who always worked there.

After the dinner, we were all shocked by Mr. Gutzlaff.

He said, "I really want to learn Japanese. I don't know how long you will stay here, perhaps at least six months. I will teach you Cantonese, so please teach me Japanese."

Six months? Our faces became pale.

"You all speak very good English. I believe you can teach me Japanese well. It is God's grace. I have always wished to learn Japanese," Mr. Gutzlaff said.

"Why do you want to learn Japanese?" I asked.

"I want to translate the Bible from English to Japanese," Mr. Gutzlaff said.

"Bible translation?" I asked.

"Yes, our Protestant church hasn't started translating the Bible in Japanese yet. I want to start while you are here. Please help me," the thirty-two-year-old Mr. Karl Gutzlaff said enthusiastically.

We didn't know how to answer. It was too dangerous a matter.

Darkness fell. After the dinner with Mr. Gutzlaff, we returned to the house next door.

Translating the Bible into Japanese was a very worrisome thing to us. There was the Foreign Exile Law in Japan.

- All Portuguese people, including the mother and all the relatives, are exiles.
- All Japanese ships and Japanese people must not leave Japan. If they speak against it, their properties and possessions are taken and they are killed.
- No one, even the noblemen or samurai, shall buy anything from foreigners.
- You shall not receive any letters from foreigners, or if the exiles come back to Japan, all their families shall be killed.
- All Christians shall be sent to jail.
- As long as the sun exists, we shall not accept any Christians. If someone is against this law, even if he is a king or a god of Christianity, he shall be beheaded.

There was the school church in Fort Vancouver.
There was the worship service on the *Eagle*.
We stayed at a pastor's house in Hawaii.
There were many churches in London.
There was Pastor Jones on the *Cambridge*.
Now we had to translate the Bible in Macao.
Can't we escape from Christianity?

"We were afraid of attending the worship service. Now we have to translate the Bible. Iwa-san, what shall we do?" I asked.

"Kenta, Kyu, I don't think Christianity is bad. What do you think?" Iwa-san asked.

"I don't think it is bad," Kyu answered.

"That is right. It's not bad. It's a very good religion. 'Humans are the same.' That was the first time I heard it. I never thought about it when I was in Japan," I said.

"Yes, Kenta, Kyu, Christianity is not bad. The Japanese officials are wrong," Iwa-san said.

"The Japanese officials are wrong?" Kyu jumped up. "Iwa-san, don't say that. You shall be killed."

"Kyu, I agree with Iwa-san. We must have a right to believe in any gods we like. Even though we pray to Jesus Christ or Buddha, there is nothing wrong with that," I said.

"Kyu, if we kill or steal, it's right to be judged. But the Japanese officials can't keep our soul. Even though we pray to Jesus Christ, the Japanese officials shouldn't kill our families. It is wrong," Iwa-san said.

"Yes, but the Japanese officials will not change the rules," Kyu said.

"That is right. They think our lives are the same as a carrot or a cabbage. We don't have to worry about the Bible translation. We learned from Pastor Jones, 'Do not be anxious about tomorrow. God will take care of your tomorrow, too. Live one day at a time.' We will help with the Bible translation," Iwa-san said.

"But if the Japanese officials hear about it?" Kyu asked.

"We are far away from Japan. They will not know it," Iwa-san said.

"I see, Iwa-san. You are brave," Kyu said.

"Anyway, Mr. Gutzlaff doesn't speak Japanese yet, so he can't translate it into Japanese soon," Iwa-san said.

"I see. By the time he learns Japanese, we will be in Japan," I said and felt relieved.

But we didn't know about Mr. Gutzlaff.

It was easy for Mr. Gutzlaff to learn foreign languages. In 1803, he was born in Prussia. He had translated the Bible into a few languages by the time he was thirty-two.

When he went to Siam (in 1949 it became Thailand), he finished translating the Bible into Siamese in nine months. He had never known Siamese before.

He believed, with John Wesley in England, that he must obey God's will even though it would be a hard thing.

Mr. Gutzlaff was excellent at time management. He didn't waste a minute, and if he wanted to do something, he tried it instantly.

His daily schedule was like this:

<u>On weekday</u>
7:00 am to 9:00 am: Old Testament Chinese translation.
9:30 am to 12:00 pm: New Testament Japanese translation.
12:00 pm to 1:00 pm: Re-examine the translation.
1:00 pm to 2:00 pm: Chinese pamphlet preparation.

2:00 pm to 5:00 pm: Study Chinese culture, visit sick people, organize the school.
6:00 pm to 10:00 pm: Writing letters or doing routine duties.

<u>On Sunday:</u>
7:00 am to 9:00 am: Old Testament Bible study in Chinese.
10:00 am to 10:30 am: Chinese worship service.
12:00 pm to 1:00 pm: Japanese worship service.
3:00 pm to 6:00 pm: Visiting Chinese people.
6:00 pm to 7:00 pm: Chinese Sunday school.
7:30 pm to 9:00 pm: The worship in the hospital.

When we saw his schedule, we were all shocked. Where did his all energy come from?

Before Mr. Gutzlaff met us, he had a Japanese-English dictionary and an English-Japanese dictionary.

He also worked as a translator at the English Department of Commerce. He earned a good income from them, but he was part-time, so he didn't have to go there every day.

~ ~ ~ ~ ~

In his youth, Karl Gutzlaff was a very romantic teenager. In 1820, he wrote a poem praising King Frederick Wilhelm III of Prussia. The king was touched by his beautiful poem, so he ordered a search for the seventeen-year-old poet.

Mr. Gutzlaff was a dreamer and an excellent poet, but he was very poor. He had to drop out of school and worked in a women's clothing shop. The officials brought the poor teenage boy before the Prussian king. After the king talked with Karl, the king ordered a scholarship for him to continue his studies. Karl Gutzlaff used his scholarship to become a missionary.

He began his missionary work in Indonesia, where he learned Chinese. He spoke fluent Chinese, wore Chinese clothes, and lived just like a Chinese man. The Chinese people called him, the Child of the Western Ocean.

~ ~ ~ ~ ~

"This is the Japanese Town," Mr. Gutzlaff said.

We saw the people, but I couldn't see any Japanese people there.

"I think there are some mixed-blood Japanese people here. The pure Japanese came here around two hundred years ago," Mr. Gutzlaff said.

"In 1614, the Tokugawa shogun ordered the Christian exile. One hundred forty-eight Christians moved to Macao and Manila. These Japanese built the St. Paul Temple. It took twenty years. But in 1613, one year before the Japanese Christians arrived here, one hundred Japanese were exiled from Macao," Mr. Gutzlaff said.

"Why?" I asked.

"There were many Japanese pirates here. Macao citizens hated the Japanese," Mr. Gutzlaff said.

"Why then did they accept these Japanese?" I asked.

"Because they were Christian," said Mr. Gutzlaff.

"Even though they were Christian, they were still Japanese," Kyu said.

"Yes, many Macao citizens didn't like the Japanese, but these Japanese lived good Christian lives, so they gained their trust," Mr. Gutzlaff said.

The stone street went uphill. Then we stopped on the stairs. There was a wall with five stairs. The rounded post held five floors. The second floor was narrower, like a triangle shape. We saw the cross on the top of the roof.

"This is the St. Paul Temple. This year, there was a fire and only this wall was left," Mr. Gutzlaff said.

"This year! That is a shame," Kyu said.

The one church wall was a striking beauty contrasting with the blue sky. I saw a few saints' statues. Then I recognized a ship. "Iwa-san, look!" I said.

"Yes, it is a ship," Iwa-san said and looked at the statue. There was a statue of St. Mary beside the ship.

There was a statue of Jesus Christ at the fourth set of stairs. But we were all interested in the ship statue. Why did they make this ship statue? They came here with a ship. If they had wanted to stay in Japan, they would have changed their religion, but they didn't. They kept their strong belief. The ship meant they had a memory of Japan, or that they wanted to go back to Japan. The Japanese built a great temple in Macao Iwa-san, Kyu, and I put our hands together and bowed.

Mr. Gutzlaff was looking at us.

Macao was a beautiful town. I saw many churches, but also Buddhist temples, too. Every time we saw the temples or churches, we put our hands together and prayed.

"I felt comfortable praying to Buddha rather than Amen," Kyu said.

When I saw the chrysanthemums and the bamboo forest, my chest hurt. *Japan is near!*

"This is the Macao mausoleum. This is god for the sailors," Mr. Gutzlaff explained.

"Oh, sailors!" we said and bowed deeply and prayed.

I looked at Mr. Gutzlaff. *Why did he never pray at any Buddhist temple? He is a strange man.*

"You pray at every temple or church. Did you pray when you were in Japan, too?" Mr. Gutzlaff asked.

We all nodded. "We are all very religious people. We were taught from our parents to pray to all gods and Buddha," I said.

Mr. Gutzlaff nodded.

I learned later. The very busy Mr. Gutzlaff took us to many churches and temples. He wanted to know the Japanese attitude toward gods in order to translate the Bible into Japanese. He tried to determine which chapter to start with.

After we got home, Mr. Gutzlaff read the New Testament, Acts 17. "Men of Athens! I see that in every way you are very religious. For as I walked around and looked carefully at your objects of worship, I even found an altar with this inscription: 'To the Unknown god.' Now what you worship as something unknown I am going to proclaim. The God who made the world and everything in it is the Lord of heaven and earth and does not live in temples built by hands," Mr. Gutzlaff said and looked at us with compassionate eyes.

I had never seen such touching eyes. I had confidence in Mr. Gutzlaff.

LOGOS

Time flew. One month had passed since we came to Macao.

We cleaned the house every day, but it was much easier than cleaning the *Eagle*.

"Ohayou gozaimasu (good morning)." We heard Japanese.

"Who is he?" we were puzzled.

Soon Mr. Gutzlaff came into the house and said, "I know my Japanese is not very good."

"You speak Japanese well," Iwa-san said in English with a smile.

He spoke good Japanese. I felt as if a Japanese man had come to our house. I didn't know he was speaking Japanese already.

In 1832, Mr. Gutzlaff spoke in Japanese with Japanese fishermen on Ryukyu Island. He also studied Japanese with a Japanese-English dictionary and an English- Japanese dictionary.

"We are going to study the Bible starting from today. Okay?" he asked and left.

"His Japanese is excellent. He could translate the Bible in Japanese by himself," Kyu commented.

After breakfast, Mr. Gutzlaff came to the room cheerfully. It was exactly 9:30 am. "As long as I stay in Macao, we will have Bible study at this time," he said.

We nodded reluctantly.

"The Bible is God's word. This is the most important book in the world," Mr. Gutzlaff said.

"Why did he say that? The Buddhist scriptures are great as well," Kyu complained in Japanese.

"Kyu, do you have any questions?" Mr. Gutzlaff asked.

"No, sir," Kyu said.

"There was a storm story in the Bible, just like you had," Mr. Gutzlaff said.

Storm stories in the Bible? My eyes were wide open.

"I am going to read Acts 27. When Paul sailed the storm came, but he saved 276 people by faith," Mr. Gutzlaff said and read the Bible slowly.

"We made slow headway for many days and had difficulty arriving off Cnidus. When the wind did not allow us to hold our course, we sailed to the lee of Crete, opposite Salome."

His English pronunciation was clear and easy to understand. I remembered that we had a storm.

"A wind of hurricane force, called the northeaster, swept down from the island. The ship was caught by the storm and could not head into the wind; so we gave way to it and were driven along. As we passed to the lee of a small island called Cauda, we were hardly able to make the lifeboat secure. When the men had hoisted it aboard, they passed ropes under the ship itself to hold it together. Fearing that they would run aground on the sandbars of Syrtis, they lowered the sea anchor and let the ship be driven along. We took such a violent battering from the storm that the next day they began to throw the cargo overboard. On the third day, they threw the ship's tackle overboard with their own hands. When neither sun nor stars appeared for many days and the storm continued raging, we gave up all hope of being saved."

Iwa-san and Kyu listened carefully. I was also straining my ears to hear. Sometimes I couldn't understand some words, but I could catch the story. Everyone had lost hope and then Paul encouraged them.

"Last night an angel of the God whose I am and whom I serve stood beside me and said, 'Do not be afraid, Paul. You must stand trial before Caesar; and God has graciously given you the lives of all who sail with you.' So keep up your courage, men, for I have faith in God that it will happen just as he told me. Nevertheless, we must run aground on some island." He kept on reading. "As Paul said, after fifteen days, they were safely on shore on the island called Malta."

"It was a very interesting story," Iwa-san said. "But it was only fifteen days. Not too bad."

Kyu and I nodded

"Yes, you sailed for fourteen months. It was a hard thing," Mr. Gutzlaff said.

"Mr. Gutzlaff, this story happened one thousand years ago. I am surprised there was a sailing ship that could carry more than two hundred people," Iwa-san said.

"Yes, it was eighteen hundred years ago, but a bigger ship existed before that. It was called Noah's Ark," Mr. Gutzlaff said.

"I know that. Dr. McLoughlin told us," Kyu said.

"But it was not a sailing ship. The ship's purpose was just to float on the water," Iwa-san said.

"Mr. Gutzlaff, do you have another ship story in the Bible?" Kyu asked.

Mr. Gutzlaff nodded, smiling, and opened the other part of the Bible.

"A long time ago, around 785 and 750 BC, before Jesus Christ was born, there was a town called Nineveh. God ordered Jonah, 'Go to the great city of Nineveh and preach against it, because its wickedness has come up before me.' But Jonah didn't obey Him. Do you know why?" Mr. Gutzlaff asked.

"Of course. If we would have gone to Edo and said, 'This town is bad, so it will be destroyed,' the Japanese officials would have put us in jail," Kyu said.

"Jonah went to Tarshish instead of Nineveh, so he went to the port and sailed the ship, but ..." Pastor Gutzlaff started to read the Bible, "Then the Lord sent a great wind on the sea, and such a violent storm arose that the ship threatened to break up. All the sailors were afraid, and each cried out to his own gods. And they threw the cargo into the sea to lighten the ship. But Jonah had gone below deck where he lay down and fell into a deep sleep. The captain went to him and said, 'How can you sleep? Get up and call on your god! Maybe he will take notice of us, and we will not perish.'"

I felt Jonah was a plucky man. *Am I able to sleep during a storm?*

He continued, "Then the sailors said to each other, 'Come, let us cast lots to find out who is responsible for this calamity.' They cast lots and the lot fell on Jonah. The sea was getting rougher and rougher. So they asked him, 'What should we do to you to make the sea calm down for us?'

"'Pick me up and throw me into the sea,' he replied, 'and it will become calm. I know that it is my fault that this great storm has come upon you.' Instead, the men did their best to row back to land. But they could not, for the sea grew even wilder than before. Then they cried to the Lord, 'O Lord, please do not let us die for taking this man's life. Do not hold us accountable for killing an innocent man, for you, O Lord, have done as you pleased.' Then they took Jonah and threw him overboard, and the raging sea grew calm." He continued, "Well, what did happen to Jonah? He was swallowed by a big fish. He stayed inside the fish for three days. Jonah asked God's forgiveness. God forgave him and ordered the fish to release Jonah. Then Jonah went to Nineveh and told them God's message."

"It is a scary story," Kyu said.

We don't want to translate the Bible into Japanese, but I feel we can't escape from Jesus Christ. The Christian God made the world; He must be powerful. God must be chasing us until we finish our duty.

"But Jonah's life was saved. So we better obey God. It must be safer," Kyu said.

~~~~~

The sea through the window was dyed red with the sunset. Winter in Macao was warm and comfortable like a greenhouse. Chrysanthemums were all over Macao.

Last September, Mrs. Gutzlaff had started the mission school. There were twelve girls and a few boys. She tried to teach like a school in England; she hired a Qing teacher and let him teach Chinese writing. Iwa-san, Kyu, and I took this class with the children.

When we arrived here, the school was on winter vacation.

A big house like a hotel. That was how I felt. I couldn't understand a school with that many beds. We couldn't imagine a boarding school. There was nothing like that in Japan.

A few days before the school started, Mrs. Gutzlaff and her nieces, Catharine and Isabella, were extremely busy preparing for the children. When the students came back, Mrs. Gutzlaff made curry rice and waited for the children. I thought all the students were rich, but most of the children's clothes were so simple or dirty. But these three women hugged each child and welcomed them. I felt they loved these children deeply. *How can they love these dirty children so much as if they were their*

Snowflake

own? We are also freeloaders, but they are very kind to us. What motivates them to act like that? I felt they were mysterious people.

Every morning, these three women helped these children wash their faces. Sometimes the children made careless mistakes. They dropped the plates and broke them. The three women took care of the children with a smile. Also, they taught the children English, math, geometry, and history. Besides, they had to do a lot of laundry. They were so energetic. Just looking at them working, I felt tired.

There were two stiff-necked boys, Harry (Catharine and Isabella's brother) and Yunin. Harry Parks became the Japanese ambassador from 1865 to 1883. Yunin went to college in America and came back to Macao. He worked for the Qing Dynasty's modernization.

Yunin was a very tiny boy. Iwa-san liked him; he must have reminded him of his son in Japan.

~ ~ ~ ~ ~

"We start the Bible translation today!" Mr. Gutzlaff said with sparkling eyes.

Finally! I sighed.

"Do you understand? No Protestant church has begun this job yet. It is a very honorable job." Mr. Gutzlaff spoke slowly and clearly. There was a thick Bible, dictionaries, notes, and several pencils on a big table.

"I chose the Gospel of John. The Gospel means good news is coming. There are four Gospels in the Bible," he said.

I remembered the message that I heard while we were on the *Cambridge.* Pastor Jones said, "They asked Jesus, 'Shall we stone the woman who had affairs?' Jesus said, 'If any one of you is without sin, let him be the first to throw a stone at her.'" This story came from the Gospel of John.

"John was Jesus Christ's disciple. His nickname was A Child of Thunder. He had a violent temper, but whether fierce or gentle, when God wants to use a person, that person works well. Now God wants to use you. Let us pray," Mr. Gutzlaff said.

I felt awed as I saw his serious eyes.

Mr. Gutzlaff prayed, "Dear Lord, we have begun to translate the Gospel of John. Thank you for revealing your will. Thank you for giving this precious task to weak servants like us. Please bless this job until we complete it. Thank you for protecting these three people with your mysterious ways. Now they are going to help me with the translation of the Bible. They are afraid of this job because of the strict Japanese rules against Christianity, but please give them peace and power. And let them understand how honorable this job is. Also please take care of their families in Japan. Someday, the Japanese will accept You, the creator of the universe, the only true God. In Jesus' name, Amen."

Mr. Gutzlaff's voice was strong, and his eyes were sparkling like two sapphires. Then he opened the Bible to the Book of Genesis and began to read. "In the beginning God created the heavens and the earth. Now the earth was formless and empty, darkness was over the surface of the deep, and the Spirit of God was hovering over the waters. And God said, 'Let there be light,' and there was light." Mr. Gutzlaff stopped reading and said, "We learned it before, didn't we?"

I nodded.

"God said, 'Let there be light,' and there was light, and God said, 'Let there be earth,' the earth was made. When God said, 'Let birds fly above the earth,' the birds flew. You must remember these things before you read the Gospel of John," he warned. Then he read from the Gospel of John. "In the beginning was the Word. Please repeat after me," he said.

So we did.

"First of all, we have to translate this. *In the beginning* means before God made the heavens and the earth in Genesis. What is the most correct word in Japanese? " Mr. Gutzlaff asked.

"The most correct word? It is difficult," Iwa-san murmured and folded his arms.

"Before the creation … it is different from many, many years ago," I said.

"How about *saisho* (at first)," Iwa-san said.

"It is not correct. There were not the best or the most," I said.

"I see. How about *hajimarini*?" Iwa-san asked.

"That is it! Iwa-san," Kyu said, clapping his hands.

"*Hajimarini*?" Mr. Gutzlaff remarked and wrote it on the note in katakana. He already knew how to write katakana. "Thank you. The next word …"

"*Word* means 'kotoba,' right?" Kyu inquired.

Mr. Gutzlaff shook his head and said, "No, this *Word* is different. I have to explain. We are talking words, but His Word is not the normal words."

It's not the normal words? I tilted my head.

"It is hard to explain. There is a Greek word, Logos. This Logos is the Word," Mr. Gutzlaff said.

We were all puzzled. He looked at us; then he wondered how he could explain. He looked at the window and thought. Three minutes passed by, then five. His face was sweating.

Why does he have such difficulty?

Mr. Gutzlaff opened his mouth. "When God made the heavens and the earth, what did he say?"

"Light!" Kyu answered with a serious tone.

"Yes, he made them with his words. The fish, birds, mountains, trees were made by the Word of his mouth. This Word is Logos. God has no body like us. God is a spirit. Well, Logos is the power to produce the heavens and the earth. Also the Word is the wisdom that can determine good or bad. Also Logos is the system, power, and wisdom that all together is the Word. This is God's sense, order, judgment of the truth, and creation."

"Iwa-san, it is hard," I said and held my head with my hands

"Indeed. It's not power or truth," Iwa-san said and sighed.

"My brain is crashing," Kyu said.

I looked at the window. I saw a blue sky like the ocean in February.

It is very difficult to translate from one language to another.

I looked at Mr. Gutzlaff. He had already translated the Bible into several languages. I felt he was a great man.

"Our monks in Japan said if we didn't know good or bad, we were called stupid men," Kyu said.

"Yes, indeed," I replied.

"Then a man who knows good or bad must be a smart man," Kyu asked.

"Yes," Iwa-san agreed.

"How about *kashikoi mono* (a smart man)?" Kyu asked.

"Wow!" we both agreed.

"*Hajimarini kashikoi mono gozaru,*" Mr. Gutzlaff said and wrote it down. "Thank you. It was the most difficult part in the Bible. We have done it. I appreciate your effort!" Mr. Gutzlaff said passionately.

"Yes, there is a proverb, 'If we start, the job is already 70 percent done.' Well, let's keep on going. This is historical work, and God is pleased with it."

This was the first day of Bible translation.

(The Gospel of John was published in Singapore in May 1837, but it did not reach Japan until 1859.)

As long as Mr. Gutzlaff was home, we worked on the Bible translation. We had only a little knowledge of Christianity, so most of the words came from Buddhism, which we learned from the monks from the Buddhist temple when we were in Japan. If we had known the word *tengoku* (heaven), we might have used it, but we didn't know the word, so we used *gokuraku* (Buddhist paradise) instead.

Mr. Gutzlaff said we must not pray to many gods. At first, I couldn't understand it. In Japan, we were taught to pray to every god except the Christian God. But now Iwa-san and I agreed that we must pray only to the one true God. I felt gods had rank just like humans had many ranks.

"Iwa-san, then is there one real God and the imitation gods in the world?" Kyu asked.

"Yes, I think so, too. Mr. Gutzlaff said the God who made this world sent Jesus Christ. If it is true, he is the only real God and other gods are not real," Iwa-san said.

"I see, if it is true, the real God will get angry when we pray to other gods," I said.

"Indeed, if a wife does not take care of her husband and loves another man, her husband must get angry," Kyu said.

"Kyu, you always think about men and women relationships, but if there is only one God, He must get upset," I said.

"Kenta, don't think too much. Sailors are always in danger, so we must pray to many gods, just in case. It is safer," Kyu said.

"Yes, but if we don't treat the real God respectfully, we must apologize," I said.

Iwa-san nodded and said, "I think praying to many gods is not a real belief. The real belief is praying to one God."

"But there are so many gods. I can't choose only one," Kyu said.

"It is difficult, but we must believe in only one God. Mr. Gutzlaff is right," Iwa-san said with a strong voice.

"Then who is the real God?" Kyu asked. "I am Japanese, so I will choose a Japanese god."

"But whether a Japanese god is a real god or not, I am not sure. Right, Iwa-san?" I asked.

Iwa-san nodded.

"Anyway, I will choose a Japanese god. How about you, Kenta?" Kyu asked.

"I don't know about one god. Because we are Japanese, we must not have favoritism," I said.

"But the real God gives orders to other gods. 'You go to Japan. You go to America,'" Kyu said.

"God's followers?" Iwa-san laughed.

"Kyu, I think the real God is the only one. Sea, mountains, stars, moon, animals, and humans were all made by the real God. Kyu, Jesus Christ died on the cross and he rose from the dead in three days. I have never heard such a story when I was in a Japanese temple," I said.

"Of course, they are not Christian," Kyu said.

"I like that story. If I believe in Jesus Christ, I will be brought up from the dark to the light," I said.

"I know, but I can't believe that Jesus rose from the dead," Iwa-san said.

"But, Iwa-san, nothing is impossible for God, right?" I asked.

"Wait! What is the difference between God and Buddha?" Kyu asked.

"It is said that Sakyamuni was a wealthy prince who had a beautiful wife. But he left his family and lived in the mountains. Then he found enlightenment under a tree. After that, he was called Buddha," Iwa-san explained.

"Then Buddha didn't make this world. He is different from God," I said.

"Well, Iwa-san, I think Mr. Gutzlaff and his family are mysterious," Kyu said.

"Why?" asked Iwa-san.

"Reading, writing, teaching, preaching are their life," Kyu said.

"Yes, indeed," Iwa-san agreed.

"He works all the time. Even Mrs. Gutzlaff takes care of Chinese children from early morning to night. She has no free time. Also young Catharine and Isabella are the same. They work all the time. What is their joy? They don't go out. Nobody orders them to work, but they keep on working," I said.

"Well, then their joy must be working," Iwa-san said.

"Working is their pleasure?" Kyu asked.

"Yes. If not, they couldn't work with such happy faces," Iwa-san said.

"Because they believe in Jesus Christ? If so, Christianity is great," I said.

"Yes, indeed," Iwa-san said.

"But when we go back to Japan, Christianity is prohibited. So we must not believe it. It's safer. I want to go back to Japan first of all. Then I will find a god," Kyu said.

"Kyu, you are right. We must not choose one god yet, even though Christianity is good," I said.

"Kyu, we saw the Slave Coast, right? Humans buy humans as if they were horses or cows. What did you feel?" Iwa-san asked.

"I felt sorry, too," Kyu said.

"But I became a slave myself, and the Hudson Bay Company set us free. Dr. McLoughlin saved us and sent us here. I won't forget his courtesy. Moreover, I saw the Slave Coast. I now really understand the slave's sadness ... Dr. McLoughlin is a true Christian," Iwa-san said. Tears dropped down from Iwa-san's big eyes.

Kyushu Men

It was December when we arrived in Macao. We had now been living in Macao for eleven months.

Our Bible translation would be done in a few days. (Gospel of John, John 1 and 2.) Mr. Gutzlaff wanted to bring this Japanese Bible to Japan.

"But it will be burned if we bring it to Japan," I said.

"Yes, I know. But God's words will remain," Mr. Gutzlaff said.

He died fifteen years later. He was forty-eight. Before he died, he quoted 1 Corinthians 15:57, "But thanks be to God! He gives us the victory through our Lord Jesus Christ." (He is still buried in Happy Valley in Hong Kong.)

~~~~~

We were cleaning the house. Catharine stood in front of our door and said, "Come. Hurry up. You have a surprise."

"Oh? Are there any beautiful women?" Kyu asked teasingly.

"No. The Japanese came," Catharine said.

"Japanese!" we shouted.

"Iwa-san! Japanese. Are there Japanese officials?" Kyu asked; his face became pale.

"Maybe," Iwa-san said with a low voice.

"My God, what can we do?" I was trembling. *We helped to translate the Bible. The Japanese officials must have discovered it.*

"Do not say anything about the Bible translation, okay?" Iwa-san ordered.

"But Mr. or Mrs. Gutzlaff might say something," I said.

"I asked them not to tell, so they will not say," Iwa-san said.

"How about Harry?" Kyu asked.

"I don't know. Harry is still a kid," Iwa-san said.

"What can we do?" Kyu asked, shaking.

We had never thought that we were afraid of Japanese people, but we are afraid of the Japanese officials.

"Hurry up! There are Japanese people who were in a storm just like you," Catharine said.

"Storm!" Kyu shouted.

They were not Japanese officials. We were relieved. We ran into the house next door; then we saw four Japanese men.

"You are Japanese!" Kyu shouted.

"Yes, you are, too!" they replied.

We looked at each other; we were speechless.

These Japanese were from Kyushu Island. They were twenty-nine-year-old Shozo, twenty-six-year-old Sabu, twenty-nine-year-old Kuma, and fifteen-year-old Riki. They left Amakusa in November 1835. Their ship carried sweet potatoes and tried to return to Nagasaki. But the storm came, and they cut down the sail. After thirty-five days, they reached Luzon Island. There was no food for thirteen days. Then they met the natives, who gave them a little food, but the natives stole all their kimonos and possessions. They lived almost naked until Spanish officials sent them to Manila. They lived in Manila for one year, but the Spanish officials didn't know what to do, so they sent them to Macao without any assistance. They had neither food nor money. They thought they would have to commit hara-kiri. Macao citizens came and asked them something, but they didn't understand the language. Then someone brought them to Mr. Gutzlaff's house. We talked about our story, too.

"You sailed fourteen months? We sailed only thirty-five days," Sabu said.

"But you didn't eat for thirteen days. That was a very hard thing. We could eat rice every day." I comforted them.

Tears fell from their eyes.

~~~~~

We were afraid of Sunday since these Kyushu men arrived in Macao. Every Sunday at noon, we attended the worship service. We were getting used to it since we had been in Fort Vancouver. But we didn't know if these Kyushu men were going to attend church or not. We were very afraid to ask them.

Mr. Gutzlaff said the night before in Japanese, "Tomorrow you go to church."

But they couldn't understand it well.

"Where do we have to go tomorrow?" Shozo asked me.

"Church. A foreign temple," Kyu said.

"A foreign temple!" Shozo repeated.

"Christian!" Kuma shouted.

"I am not sure, but it may be Christian. But we are not Christian. They give us room and board, so we just attend as an obligation," Kyu explained.

Shozo nodded and said, "I understand. Until we go back to Japan, we will follow their rules."

Shozo is an understanding man.

"Christianity is fearful. Japanese officials will kill us! You must be Christian!" Kuma yelled.

Iwa-san shook his head and said, "Of course not. We want to go back to Japan as soon as possible. Why should we be Christians?"

"Yes, Iwa-san is right. We stayed with the English, so we learned their language. That is all. We are not Christians," Kyu commented.

"Our wish is only to go back to Japan. We are not Christian," I said, too.

"I am sorry Kuma said something rude," Shozo said politely; then the four of them talked. People from Kyushu Island spoke a different dialect. Their words were like a foreign language. Shozo and Sabu knew both standard Japanese and the Kyushu dialect well. When they spoke to us, they spoke clear standard Japanese. Mr. Gutzlaff became confused when he heard the Kyushu dialect.

I was worried about the Bible translation. If the Kyushu men found out that we helped with the Bible translation, what would they think?

On the first Sunday since these Kyushu men had arrived, Iwa-san, Kyu, and I were nervous, but the seven Japanese marched to the small church.

We all sat on the bench in the church. Catharine stood by the organ and smiled at us. The organ played and then Mr. Gutzlaff read the Japanese Bible, which we translated. He read 1 John 2:2, "He is the atoning through sacrifice for our sins, and not only for ours, but also for the sins of the whole world." Mr. Gutzlaff smiled and said, "I am very happy today. I can pray with seven Japanese people."

He must have been glad he was able to read the Japanese Bible to seven Japanese so soon.

"We all have sins. Hate, bitterness are sins as well. Our hearts have sins every day, so we deserve go to hell," Mr. Gutzlaff said.

Kuma covered his ears with his hands, but Shozo, Sabu, and Riki listened silently.

"Our sins destroy us, but there is only one way that we can avoiding going to hell. Jesus Christ shed his blood for us, so if we believe in Jesus Christ, we will be saved. Do not forget. Do you have sins?" Mr. Gutzlaff asked in Japanese.

"Yes, our ship was drifting; that was a big sin," Shozo said.

"Drifting?" Mr. Gutzlaff was puzzled.

"In Japan, the Japanese officials don't put us in a jail even though we hate or say bad things, but once we drift and go back to Japan, we have to go in a jail and sometimes we will be killed. Drifting is a big sin," Shozo said.

"Oh, no, it's not sin. Our hearts make sins: hatred, jealousy, stealing someone's husband or a wife—such things are humans' sins, so the Bible tells us. But Jesus Christ died for our sins. We are safe now," Mr. Gutzlaff said.

"It is a lie. Die for our sins? I can't believe it!" Sabu shouted.

Why can't you believe it? Jesus Christ died for our sins! I shouted in my heart; then I was shocked at my thought.

Going Home

The English officials found a ship for us. It was the *Morrison*, an American ship. We were relieved and already dreaming about Japan. I imagined when the *Morrison* reached Onoura Beach, my hometown, people might be surprised when they saw the big ship. When they saw us, they may think we were ghosts. They might have built our gravestones.

Is my father still alive? How about my mother and my sister? Is Yuki married already? When I thought about Yuki, my heart sank.

Once we were told that the Qing ship would take us to Japan because the Qing Dynasty and Japan had trade, but the Qing Dynasty knew about the Japanese officials' strict rules about drifting on the sea; the Qing Dynasty refused to bring us to Japan.

Official letters went back and forth several times from London to Macao, because we were still under the control of English officials. It took a few months to receive one letter. So we had to stay in Macao more than one year.

On July 4, 1837, the seven Japanese men were on the *Morrison*. Captain James had decided to remove the cannons from the *Morrison* in order to make a good impression on the Japanese officials.

On July 12, 1837, the *Morrison* lowered the ship's anchor in Naha in Ryukyu Island. I saw Japanese ships just like the *Takaramaru*.

"Look, Iwa-san!" I shouted as if I were a kid.

"Japan is near!" Iwa-san said and breathed deeply.

The Ryukyu officials came to the *Morrison* and recommended that we sail on the Japanese ship to Japan. But we knew now the differences between the Japanese ship and these English or American ships. We were afraid of depending on the Japanese ship. What if we were to have a storm and drift again? We decided to go back to Japan with the *Morrison*. Iwa-san told our decision to Captain James. The captain nodded and understood our feelings.

On July 25, the *Morrison* couldn't sail because the very strong southwest current obstructed the way. They tried to go ahead the next day, but they were still not able to sail.

"If the ship goes closer to land, we will ride on the northeast current," Iwa-san suggested.

Captain James followed Iwa-san's advice; then the *Morrison* could sail fifty-three miles a day. Kyu and I were very proud of Iwa-san. I was very glad. If Iwa-san had not been with us, we would not have been able to reach Japan. But the captain was great and humble because he followed Iwa-san's advice.

On July 29, Japan, a beautiful country with greenery and mountains, jumped into view.

"Oh, Japan!" the seven Japanese men said; everyone's eyes were wet with tears.

We were of course happy to see our families, but also we were afraid of the Japanese officials.

"How long will the Japanese officials check us?" Kyu asked.

"I heard for six months," I said.

"Six months?" asked Kyu.

"One of the sailors told me before. In 1805, a Japanese man whose name was Matsujiro sailed from Osaka to Hawaii. An American ship sent him back to Japan, but the Japanese officials treated him very harshly and he became insane and hung himself," Shozo said.

"It was pitiful. Why did Japanese officials examine him so hard?" I asked.

"I don't know, but the Japanese officials would ask, 'Where did you meet the storm? Which country saved you? Was there any trade during the trip? Are there any guns? Did you become Christian?'" Shozo said.

"Will they ask if we learned about Christianity?" Kyu asked.

"I think so, but we have to say we didn't hear anything about Christianity, but Riki is still a child, so I am afraid it will slip his lips," Shozo said.

We were worried, too. We couldn't imagine what kind of method the Japanese officials would use. If the Japanese officials found a sinner, it would be to their credit. So in order to have great exploits, they would be skillful. If something bad happened after we were released, it would be the Japanese officials' responsibility, so they took their time.

We didn't become Christian, but we attended Christian churches. Will we able to endure the Japanese officials' torture?

~~~~~

"What a beautiful country! Mountains and mountains. Look at Mount Fuji," Mr. Gutzlaff said.

"Indeed! We are looking at a panorama," Captain James said.

"We can't describe this beauty with a mouth or pen. Now I understand why Iwa-san and Shozo are such honorable people," Mr. Gutzlaff said.

"The Japanese officials will accept us kindly. They may trade with America," Captain James said.

"I hope so, too," Mr. Gutzlaff said.

~~~~~

Yes, our home country Japan was beautiful, but the Japanese isolationism was strong.

We had decided to go to Edo. The captain brought a letter that told about seven drifted Japanese and the history of America. He also brought gifts, which were George Washington's portrait, a pair of gloves, an encyclopedia, a telescope, an American history book, an American treaty, and many kinds of medicines.

The Morrison *wouldn't cause any harm to Japan. The cannons are out and there are no Christian flyers. They are just trying to send us back to Japan. I hope the Japanese officials accept us.*

On July 30, 1837, the Morrison was closer to Edo. It was a chilly summer. We saw many Japanese fishing boats under the cold rain. They seemed to ignore the *Morrison*.

At noon, we heard a big sound.

"What is it?" Iwa-san asked and strained his ears.

"It must be thunder," Kyu said.

We heard the sound again.

"It's thunder," Riki said.

"No, it is a cannon," Shozo said.

"Cannon!" everyone said.

"I used to hear the cannon's sound," Shozo said.

"The cannon is used for war," Kyu said.

"Of course," Shozo replied.

They stopped eating lunch and went to the deck. The sailors tried to change the position of the sails.

Then we heard the sound, again.

"What kind of sound is it?" Captain James asked.

"Cannon," Iwa-san said; his eyes became dark.

"Hmm … do you have such experience, captain?" Mr. Gutzlaff asked.

The captain shook his head and said, "Iwa-san and Shozo are very well-mannered people. I think the Japanese must be saluting. So this must be salutes to welcome the *Morrison.*"

"I see; it is a relief," Mr. Gutzlaff said.

"What do you think?" Iwa-san translated the captain and Mr. Gutzlaff's conversation to Shozo.

"I have never heard about a salute," Shozo replied.

Iwa-san nodded and told it to Captain James.

"I see. If it is not a salute, it must be a signal," Captain James said.

"Iwa-san, we must put up an American flag," Kyu suggested.

"That is a good idea. The Japanese officials know the English and the Dutch flags, but they don't know the American flag. So they may treat us differently. America has never been an enemy to Japan," Mr. Gutzlaff said.

Soon an American flag was flying from the top of the mast.

The sound of gunfire was increased.

"Oh!" Kuma shouted. Half a mile ahead of the *Morrison,* a black thing fell into the sea and then a column of water arose.

"Artillery! It's not a salute," the captain shouted and bit his lip.

"Can't they see this America flag? Iwa-san!" Kyu said.

But Iwa-san didn't answer. His cheeks twitched. The cannons kept on firing. A shot fell by Iwa-san's feet.

"Iwa-san!" everyone shouted. An artillery shell bounced and fell down into the sea.

"Are you okay, Iwa-san?" I asked.

"I am fine. The Japanese cannon ball doesn't explode," he said with a low voice.

"I am glad. I thought you died," I said and rubbed Iwa-san's feet.

Kyu's face became like an oni (Japanese monster), and he yelled, "Iwa-san, a Japanese cannon shot you! A Japanese cannon!"

Iwa-san was silent and went back to work.

Ka-boom, ka-boom! One after another, the cannon balls flew toward the *Morrison*. It was noisy enough to burst our eardrums. Then a few Japanese warships attacked us.

Thirty or forty samurais were on each ship.

"Beast! You still try to shoot us!" Shozo shouted, grinding his teeth.

Soon the *Morrison* and the Japanese ship were far apart. We heard the Japanese samurais shout their victory.

The captain and the sailors regretted not bringing their cannons.

But Mr. Gutzlaff said, "It was good that the *Morrison* removed the cannons. If we had the cannons, we would have had to shoot back. Yes, if we had a sword, we would have been destroying with a sword."

What should we do now? I looked toward Edo, and soon Edo disappeared. Tears dropped from my cheeks as if they were waterfalls.

Japan closed the country in 1825, because of an incident with an English ship.

In October 1808, an English ship, the *Felton*, came to Nagasaki with Dutch flags. At that time, Holland and China traded with Japan. The *Felton* was looking for the two Dutch ships. The two Japanese officials welcomed the *Felton* without any doubt. The captain caught these two Japanese officials as hostages and checked if two Dutch ships were in the Nagasaki port. Moreover, three English boats inspected the port. There were no Dutch ships in the port. The captain returned one hostage and asked for water and food to be supplied. "If you don't obey our request, we will burn all the ships in the port," the captain said.

The Nagasaki magistrate, Matsudaira Yasuhide, was angry at the English, so he ordered the *Felton* be burned. But the Nagasaki guard didn't have strong defenses. After the war ended, there continued an era of peace. The Nagasaki guard wasn't prepared for the fight; the

Nagasaki magistrate accepted the English request. The *Felton* returned the hostage and left Nagasaki victorious.

After that, the Nagasaki magistrate, Matsudaira Yasuhide, felt responsible and committed hara-kiri. His chief retainers also followed him and died. But we didn't know about such matters at that time.

~ ~ ~ ~ ~

No one had any energy left to speak.

Why can't we just go home? We were so happy going back to Japan. But our dreams have been destroyed.

"We better die," someone murmured.

I nodded. I looked around. Iwa-san was not in the cabin. He must be very disappointed. Last night he smiled and said, "My son, Iwataro, must be half my height."

Will Iwa-san jump into the sea? I felt uneasy. *If Iwa-san dies, I will die, too.* I stood up.

"Where are you going?" Kyu asked.

"I will look for Iwa-san. He may be thinking about suicide," I said.

Kyu nodded and said, "Kenta, if Iwa-san dies, I will die, too." Kyu stood up.

Then Shozo opened his eyes big and said, "We will die together."

Then Sabu, Kuma, and Riki said, "I will die."

"I will, too …"

After the *Morrison* was shot, we forgot to eat and we were all out of our minds. The word *die* was the first thing that came out from our mouths. We all stood up, and then the door opened and Iwa-san came into the cabin. He must have felt despair.

"Where are you going?" Iwa-san asked.

"We were coming to see you," I said.

Iwa-san looked puzzled.

"We thought you might die. So we were going to die with you," Shozo said.

"Is that true?" Iwa-san asked and sat on the floor.

"Iwa-san, what were you thinking while you stood on the deck?" Kyu asked.

"Death," Iwa-san said.

"I see," Kyu said.

"I wished to see my parents, wife, and son. I just hoped to see them again. I think you are all thinking the same," Iwa-san said.

"Sailors are often out to the sea. So we live peacefully together," Shozo said.

"Yes, as long as we could eat under the one roof, we were happy," Iwa-san said.

"Yes, but we lost the hope of going back to Japan. Even if we went back to Macao, what kind of lives would be waiting for us?" Shozo asked.

"Yes, indeed. I don't want to live in a foreign country anymore," Kuma said.

"Yes, but not only that. I feel ashamed of the Japanese rudeness. Mr. Gutzlaff and the captain removed the cannons. As I am Japanese, I want to ask forgiveness for the Japanese officials' bad behavior," Iwa-san said.

"I see. We must commit hara-kiri and ask for forgiveness," Shozo said.

"I think so. Moreover, they tried to send us to Japan; then they have to take us back to Macao. It is too much burden for them," Iwa-san said.

They became silent.

Mr. Gutzlaff said, "We were shot at for one hour but no one was hurt. It was a miracle. Let's pray."

Then they prayed thankfully. I was shocked. Under any circumstances, they were grateful. Even the sailors patted our shoulders and comforted us. I didn't think they would think we were a nuisance, but Iwa-san's words were right. We had lost all hope now. It was time to die.

"Iwa-san, how can we die?" I asked.

"Yes, hanging is not beautiful. Even to jump in the sea is not perfect. Someone may save us. If we commit hara-kiri, the ship gets dirty. But if I am the only one who dies, that will be enough," Iwa-san said; his eyes became soft and looked at me.

"No, I want to die, too," Riki cried.

Then everyone started to cry.

We all felt that our home country had thrown us away. We were very lonely, and our wailing filled the cabin.

"Suicide! Oh, no!" Mr. Gutzlaff shouted and ran into the cabin.

"But, Mr. Gutzlaff, the Japanese officials shot cannons. It's shameful. I am sorry. We want to die for the pardon," Iwa-san said.

"It's pitiful!" Mr. Gutzlaff said. "Iwa-san, I understand your feelings, but suicide is a sin. God will not be pleased. The Japanese officials' sin must be paid by them.

You didn't shoot, but they did."

"But I am very ashamed. We are also Japanese. How can we ask for your forgiveness. You are so kind, but not the Japanese officials," Iwa-san said.

"It's not your fault. Maybe an American whaling ship did something wrong, so they fear us. Even though they shot at us, we must not give up yet. We have to pray and try it again," Mr. Gutzlaff said. "We must find a port without cannons." He smiled at us.

After discussing it, we tried to go to Toba, which was very close to Onoura; but with a strong wind against us, we couldn't reach it. Iwa-san, Kyu, and I were disappointed. Then the Kyushu men suggested going to the domain of Satsuma in Kyushu. Satsuma had authority not only over Kyushu but also Ryukyu and Taiwan.

"The Qing ship and Dutch ships come to Kagoshima," Shozo said.

"Oh! Foreign ships go to Kagoshima?" Captain James asked.

"Yes, they sell merchandise, secretly," Mr. Gutzlaff said.

"Well, does Satsuma trade with the Dutch and Qing without the shogun's permission?" Captain James asked.

"I heard they do," Mr. Gutzlaff said.

~ ~ ~ ~ ~

On August 10, 1837, the *Morrison* was headed toward Kagoshima Island. Cape Kagoshima was beautiful in the morning sun.

"I miss it!" Sabu shouted.

The captain dropped the anchor. As Shozo suggested, Shozo, Sabu, and a few sailors tried to search for the town; they launched a small boat and left.

"Are they safe, Iwa-san?" I asked, looking at the boat.

"I don't know," Iwa-san said.

After we had lived in foreign countries for five years, we had learned to respect every individual. I had an idea that if we talked to them, the

Japanese officials would understand us, but Japanese and Westerners were very different. I found that out when they shot at our ship.

We worried about Shozo and Sabu. *If they were beaten …* Our faces grew pale.

Four hours passed, and then the small boat came closer to the *Morrison*. We saw that Shozo waved from the boat. *They are safe!*

Shozo told us he had met the Nagasaki officials and told them his story. They showed deep sympathy. The Nagasaki officials wanted to see Iwa-san in order to hear his story.

So the next day, Iwa-san and Shozo went together to meet them.

Several officials sat on stools. Iwa-san and Shozo sat on the ground, and many residents stood surround them.

"Hmm … such a huge wave that came straight at your ship. It was a miracle you did not sink," the Nagasaki official said.

"Yes, we prayed to Funadama-san, cut the mast … we worked together," Iwa-san explained.

"Then what happened?" the official asked.

"Sea, sea, sea. We had neither water nor vegetable. We became slaves," Iwa-san said.

Some residents sobbed.

When Iwa-san told them about England, they didn't know where England was. He also told about the Hudson Bay Company's kindness.

"Hmm … the foreigners took care of you in such a kind way. Are they humans like us?" the official asked.

"Yes, indeed. Perhaps greater than humans," Iwa-san said.

"I think so. They must be the gods or Buddha. Normal people don't show such kindness," said the official.

Iwa-san told how the *Morrison* had removed the cannons, but Japanese samurais still shot at us. We had thought about committing hara-kiri.

The Nagasaki officials shed their tears.

"It was cruel!" the residents shouted.

"Shooting a foreign ship is a law in Japan, but if they had known there were Japanese on the ship, they wouldn't have shot at the *Morrison*," one of the Nagasaki officials said compassionately. "You want to see your families, don't you?"

"Yes, in order to see my family, I would endure anything," Iwa-san replied.

Then a middle-aged man spoke up, "I heard you ate well. Why do you come back to Japan while we are suffering from a famine?"

"Oh, yes," added a young official. "In Osaka, there was a rice strike. Many people died without food. There are many beggars here, too. Why do you come back at such a difficult time?"

"Shut up! They went though many hardships. Don't you understand their feelings? Family is most important. They are valuable!" the older official reproached the younger official. Then he looked at Iwa-san and said, "I wrote down everything you said. I will send this document to our lord as soon as possible. You may go home soon without any punishment, but you are not Christian, are you?"

"No, I am not. I prayed to Japanese gods every day," Iwa-san answered. Both Iwa-san and Shozo bowed deeply.

"I see. As long as you are not Christians, you will have no problems. Japanese people must go back to Japan. Wait patiently for our answer. We will give you a response in three days," the official said.

Iwa-san and Shozo bowed and cried.

The residents cheered and said to the Nagasaki officials, "Please let them go home!"

"Don't worry. Meeting the storm was not your sin. The lord of Satsuma is a open-minded man. I believe our lord will allow you to stay in Japan. Please wait for three days," the official said; his voice was filled with compassion.

Iwa-san and Shozo came back to the *Morrison*.

After we heard their story, we clapped our hands as if we were already at home.

"We can go home!"

"Father! Mother! I can see you soon!"

"Wait three days!"

Our joy filled the cabin.

But we didn't know Captain James received the statement that Iwa-san had given to the Nagasaki officials. When they tried to send it to their lord, the chief officials refused it. They promised that some officials would come to receive these seven Japanese men and their document soon.

August 12, 1837, was a cold drizzling day.

"This will be our last day on the *Morrison*. Don't forget to express thanks and clean the cabin neatly," Iwa-san ordered.

"Oh, yes!" we responded happily.

Iwa-san and I went to the deck. White waves broke against the rocks. Seagulls flew low over the sea. I saw green rolling hills surrounding the village.

"We can sleep in the Japanese graveyard someday," Iwa-san said peacefully.

We waited for the Nagasaki officials. They said they would pick us up in three days. Near the shore, a few surveillance ships rocked gently on the sea.

"Oh! What is that?" Kyu asked.

A boat came closer. We thought it would be the Nagasaki officials, but instead we saw three fishermen. I was disappointed. The fishing boat came up to the right side of the *Morrison* so the surveillance ships couldn't see it. I waved. Mr. Gutzlaff and the captain came up on the deck, too.

"We are going fishing," one man shouted to us.

"Fishing? The waves are so high," Iwa-san said.

"Yes, but we are used to such waves," the man said.

"Can you stay here a while?" Iwa-san asked.

"We want to, but we are prohibited to come close to any foreign ships. So we must look at the huge ship from here," the man said.

"Okay. Do you know if any Nagasaki officials are coming?" Iwa-san asked.

"Well, there is a rumor that the Nagasaki officials are not coming, and ..." the man said.

"And what?" asked Iwa-san.

"It is very hard to tell you, but your ship will be attacked by cannons," the man said.

"Cannons! Are they really going to shoot us? Tell me it's a joke," said Iwa-san.

The three fishermen were silent. Then the oldest man said, "I feel sorry for you. But it's not a joke. I am telling the truth."

"Then the officials will shoot us again?" Iwa-san asked.

The three men looked at Iwa-san.

"Liar! The Nagasaki officials said we could go home," Iwa-san said.

"No! You can't go home. I am sorry; this is no lie," the man said.

Mr. Gutzlaff translated their conversation to the captain.

"Who said such a thing?" Iwa-san said.

There was no answer.

"Who said?" Iwa-san shouted again.

The three men muttered to each other; then one man said, "Nobody said. This is a rumor in the village."

"Oh, just a rumor," Iwa-san said and was relieved.

"I know the story. At first our village residents and the officials thought a war ship came; now we understand that the ship brought you. We all have sympathy for you; but you'd better sail before the cannons begin to fire," the man said.

"What? Did the Nagasaki officials tell you this?" Iwa-san asked.

But they didn't answer and left.

Mr. Gutzlaff and the captain decided the fishermen seemed unsure of their story, so the captain ignored it and left the deck.

~~~~~

"Oh! Look!" I shouted. There were the blue and white curtains on the beach.

"It means war," Iwa-san said, his face blue like the dark sea.

We ran to the cabin. Everyone was busy cleaning in the cabin.

"We can't go home," Iwa-san said.

"Why?" Shozo asked.

"They will shoot us. Three fishermen told us," Iwa-san said.

"No!" Kuma shouted.

"Will they shoot us again?" asked Shozo.

"I want to go home!" Riki yelled.

Everyone started to cry.

"I must tell the captain about the curtains that mean war," Iwa-san said and left the cabin.

I can't believe it! Why will they shoot us again! I bit my lip. I felt blood run down and wet my jaw.

Cannons began to fire. The *Morrison* raised the sea anchor, but the wind dropped; it was high tide. Many rocks made it very dangerous to sail. The sailors endured but then got angry as they tried to escape the rocks. The *Morrison* rode the ebbing tide. Samurais and residents watched the *Morrison* from the shore. When the ship headed to the west, cannon fire came from the west coast, and when the *Morrison* went to the east, the east coast cannons fired.

At 3:00 pm, the *Morrison* finally escaped.

Iwa-san, Kyu, and I stood on the deck. We still saw the fire from the distance.

"Stop shooting!" Kyu shouted with tears.

"The Japanese officials chased us out of Japan, Iwa-san," I said.

"Yes, they discarded us, but there is someone who never betrayed us," Iwa-san said.

"Yes, God saved us through Dr. McLoughlin, Mr. Gutzlaff, the English officials, Mr. Bacon, and many other people," I said.

I hope no one ever experiences suffering like ours!

The cannons went on firing as if they were still threatening us.

Sayonara, Japan ... My eyes were wet with new tears and my sight was blurred.

Epilogue

On August 12, 1837, the *Morrison* left Cape Kagoshima, and returned to Macao on August 29, 1837.

The men from Kyushu lived in Macao. Kuma died of disease, and Sabu died of opium addiction.

Riki moved to Hong Kong and worked at a newspaper company. As he was young, he easily learned English. In September, 1855, he visited Nagasaki as a translator. When he went to Nagasaki, he wanted to live with his mother, and asked the Nagasaki officials, but they didn't permit it. He later went to Hakodate and told his story to the Hakodate officials. Eventually, he married an American woman, and they had three children.

Shozo lived in Macao and taught Japanese. A few years later, he moved to Hong Kong and opened a tailor shop; his business went well. He married a Chinese woman and they had one son. He grew wealthy and hired many servants. He and his wife had a happy marriage. They cared for shipwrecked Japanese people.

Iwa-san worked at an English-managed office as a translator with Mr. Gutzlaff. His married life was not happy, probably because he still loved his Japanese wife, Akiko. He died in June, 1852. He was only forty-eight years old.

Kyu worked with Iwa-san as a translator. He married a Chinese woman and had children.

I worked as a sailor on the *Morrison,* and I sailed to America. Captain James died two months after we arrived in Macao. His health was greatly weakened by the pressure and responsibility he endured during the escape from Kagoshima. I worked on war ships and also merchant ships. Later I moved to Shanghai and was employed by the Dent Commercial Firm. I married an English woman, but soon after we married, she died. Then I married a Malayan woman. She reminded me of my first love, Yuki. We had two sons and a daughter. We were a very close family. My wife was a good person. She could speak Japanese. We often traveled together.

In 1849, I sailed to Japan on the English warship, *Marina*. I was a translator.

In 1854, a Japanese-English Peace Treaty was passed, and I was at the Nagasaki magistrate's house as a translator.

Once in a while, Japanese refugees stayed at my house. I always remembered my own experience as a refugee. I tried to comfort them.

In 1862, I moved to my wife's hometown, Singapore. God blessed me and my family.

Acknowledgments

I want to give a special word of thanks to many of my friends.

Members of the Virginia Beach Writers and Hampton Roads Writers always gave me good advice.

Thank you to my dear friends Mary Ellen Legg, Kay Brownlow, Valerie Wilkinson, Jill Burr, Larry Elliot, John Marken, Anne Meek, Lib Conner, Dr. Jerome W. Schonefeld, and Rev. Harold Burchett, who read my entire manuscript and gave me excellent guidance.

Thank you to LCDR Ed DeLong, who provided me with ship information.

Thank you to my writing teachers, Lauran Straight, Dr. David G. Clark, Ned McIntosh, Claire Smith, Judy Tressel, Lester Atkins, and especially Ed Bacon.

Also thank you for the prayers of my Virginia Beach Community Chapel friends, especially Gaile Turnbull.

Thank you to Yoshiko Z. Jaeggi, who made the cover art.

And I appreciate the encouragement and excellent suggestions of Laura Arnold.

Finally, thank you to iUniverse that made my book.

Without your help, I couldn't have completed this book.
I hope the Lord will use this book to His glory.